MW01616514

WHEN A WOMAN'S FED UP

**(Sequel to
Do You Really Know Your Man)**

A James Hickman Book

**Bent Publishing
Atlanta, Ga.**

ISBN#: 978-1-4243-3384-4

Cover by: www.MarionDesigns.com
Author photo: Dennis Byron
Editor: Elnora Daugherty

Printed in the United States of America

Published by
Bullet Entertainment Group
5441 Riverdale Rd. Suite 129
College Park, Ga 30349
www.Bentpublishing.com
Email: bulletent4000@yahoo.com

To order additional copies wholesale, please contact James Hickman at 404-246-6496 or bulletent4000@yahoo.com

WHEN A WOMAN'S FED UP

Also By James Hickman...

Do You Really Know Your Man?
Out Of the Game
What People do For Money
No Good Baby Daddy (June '07)
Wolf In Sheep Clothing (July '07)
Games Men Play (July '07)
Love Triangle (August '07)
Between Two Sisters (October '07)
Official Contact Pages/Self Publishing
Official Contact Pages/The Music Industry
Official Contact Pages/The Music Industry Dictionary

ACKNOWLEDGEMENTS

First of all, I give thanks to God for having a son like Jesus watching over me all the way, and for being there for me, when I was down in out. Thank you, Lord!

I also give thanks to my Mom, Mary Stewart; my children Decarol, Jamarco, Frankie, James; and my brothers, Anthony, Ira, Tracy and Grady.

CHAPTER 1

Six months passed since Dolorian saw her girls. They all parted going there separate ways after their vacation in the Caribbean together. A girls night out was in order and just what Dolorian needed it. To finally see the faces of the ones she could tell her deepest secrets too. Sakina, Dia, Destini, was all she could think about while driving down highway 85 in her brand new candy apple red BMW truck. She left one of her favorite spots, Peppers bar and Grill where she and the bartender G have an understanding. As soon as the bartender saw Dolorian's face in the crowd he whipped up her favorite drink "A woman's revenge", he pulled out the bottle of Kaluha and lime juice, placing a ½ shot of each in her glass.

"I got your favorite, baby; bring your fine ass over here!" G yelled across all the music, and loud laughing going on.

Dolorian played back each step she took while in Peppers Bar and Grill. Until she laid eyes on Marcus, Dia's ex-man. This was the last face she expected to see in the crowd. Him and his boy's hugged up on some south side ho's. This made her hot to see him, after all the pain and mental anguish he caused her girl Dia. Dolorian ducked and dodged her way out the door, not wanting to be seen by him. She knew if his bull shittin and signifying career of using woman was ever going to end she would have to be the one to initiate it. Dia would never have enough backbone to carry out such a scheme. Dolorian knew she was the strongest Diva in the bunch, after all she had expertise after stripping for four years, of what a man wanted and what men needed. She planned on using this skill to bring Marcus, K-Killa, Wallace and Boo to their knees and make them beg for mercy if she had anything to do with it.

Dolorian giggled to herself as she maneuvered her high maintenance automobile through the streets of ATL. The traffic was thick as usual on a Friday night and the music filled the air while the tourist and Georgian residence filled the sidewalks as well as the streets. Each club she passed was jamming, but this was the last thing on Dolorian's mind. She thought how K-Killa's wife couldn't even suck him right, but yet she got to live in a Spanish Villa on the beaches of Miami with his baby on her hip while K-Killa went around playing with single women hearts, one being hers. Jealousy overpowered Dolorian like never before. She felt betrayed, abandoned, and worst of all used up by a man she thought loved her. She had to come up with a way to get even if it was the last thing she did on this earth. What ever the plan, she knew her girls would back her up one hundred percent, without getting their hands dirty. All she had to do was say the word and it was on.

Sakina paced the floor of her big empty house after Wallace packed up his shit and left her to move in with his lover, with the big black dick. All the while leaving her boiling in the spot of uncertainties. She cried as she held the big white envelope up to her heart, which contained the results of the test that would change her life as she knew it. She needed her girls more than ever at this moment, but communication wasn't one of her strong points; She thought about how she drove Wallace away by not communicating with him, but she hated the fact that Wallace was the type of man that never really gave a fuck about her, after he stood in front of a preacher and said "I do". All he ever wanted was a big black dick penetrating his ass hole from the start. This brought tears to Sakina's eyes just thinking about her man making love to his boyfriend, while she stood in the middle of the floor holding on to the aids test that would make her or break her.

Dolorian opened her baby phat phone case and dialed each one of her friend's numbers to set up and appointment to do brunch, lunch or dinner, which ever one they would be available for. "Hello" Dolorian said into the phone waiting for a response.

"Who's this?" Sakina ask with big raindrop tears flowing down her cheeks as feelings of depression took over.

"Hay girl, long time no hear. I was hoping we could all get together at the Cheesecake factory tomorrow, since we haven't seen each other since the Caribbean". Dolorian smiled not knowing the state of mind her long time friend was in after the tragic break up and broken marriage.

"Are you alright, Sakina?" Dolorian asks not understanding the agony Sakina was going through.

"I just received the test back from the clinic." Sakina answered in a soft voice as she sniffled.

"Oh, baby, I'll be right there. Just hold on, Sakina I'm coming!" Dolorian answered as her BMW trucked passed by all kinds of cars, trucks, and SUV cursing to herself about Wallace and the death sentence he left behind as a good bye gift to her girl Sakina.

Dolorian called Dia hoping they would be able to make it to her girl's night out.

"Hello?" Dia ask when she answered the phone from her desk of one of the high powered Real Estate agency in Mid Town Georgia she thought this transfer was necessary after being sexually humiliated by Marcus and Rod his homeboy that meant more to him than she.

"It's me Dia. I was just calling to see if you can hook up tomorrow night at the Cheese cake factory. I have something I want to tell you and you're not going to like it." Dolorian said with the sarcasim that she was so famous for.

"Why wait, tell me now? Does it have something to do with Sakina?" Dia asks as she worked on a deal she was closing. She had been very fortunate since she threw herself into her work after she and Marcus departed on fucked up terms.

"I saw Marcus. And you'll never believe where." Dolorian exposed like an open sore.

"Where did you see that scoundrel?' Dia asks with a slight angry look on her face.

"Him and his boy Rod was hugged up on some of those south side ho's. They were at Pepper's Bar and Grill. I didn't want to be seen so I ducked and dodged out the back door. G was kind enough to let me out. Girl, I wanted to give that nigga a piece of my mind but then I started thinking, we are going to give him Wallace and K-Killa and Boo a taste of their own medicine. There is no way we're going to sit back act like a kept woman." Dolorain explained, as her mouth ran ten miles per hour. But each word that came out made a lot of sense. She was a sure enough mastermind when it came to making a man beg, Dia thought as she listened in on what Dolorian was saying.

"Did you tell Sakina or Destini yet? Dia asks waiting patiently for the answer as she continued to write, wearing her ear piece to continue their conversation.

"No, Sakina is going crazy over there in that big ass house all by herself, who would have even known. She doesn't want to call a nigga when she needs support. She just received her aids test back you know. Do you think she has it? Dolorian asked Dia.

"There is no telling. I thought my situation with my man was bad, damn she has it worst of all. Shit, then again after the shit Marcus and

Rod did to me I need to go get tested myself." Dia said.

"You haven't been tested? Girl after all those nigga's gangbanged you? There is no way. How could you wait so long?" Dolorian asked with surprise in her voice.

"I was scared. If I go to the clinic and they tell me I have that shit there is no telling what I'll do. I've already went out and bought a gun. If I see Marcus I might kill him!" Dia said breaking out of her shell for a minute Her voice was so loud it carried over to the office next to hers, sparking suspicion in the air.

"I have a plan. I want revenge for all the shit K-Killa did to me. Making love to me on the regular then gets up and leaves. There's no telling how many bitches he's shacked up with in a twenty four hour period, after all he loves to sling dick." Dolorian said as she pulled into Sakina driveway.

"I'll call you back later. I just pulled into Sakina's driveway. There is no telling what I'm going to see when I knock on the door. She sounded pretty horrible on the phone." Dolorian said as she parked the truck and picked up her Prada bag throwing it on her shoulders. She turned around to make sure her doors were locked. She pointed the little black alarm system towards the car locking her doors and turning off the lights. Sakina's door opened but no one was standing there. Dolorian walked up to the door and pushed it all the way open. She found Sakina sitting on the couch holding the test still unopened and a box of Kleenex tissue sat on the coffee table in front of her, along with a bottle of patron and a bottle of pills.

"What the fuck is going on here?" Dolorian asked as she noticed the suicide kit sitting on the table. "I know your not in here taking pills with liquor are you trying to kill your self or something, girl." Dolorian moved the bottle of pills checking out the label before doing so.

"What's really going on with you Sakina? How come you haven't called? If the shit Wallace did to you is making you break down like this, we are going to have to do something about it, Dolorian said as she reached over to give Sakina a big hug. "That's one of the reason's I called you."

Sakina hand Dolorian the aids test asking her to open it. Reading what was inside the big white envelope. Dolorian eyes widen to think she would be the first one to know the answer to the question that's been on all their minds ever since Sakina told them Wallace had a boyfriend.

"Is that no good nigga here?" Dolorian asked, not knowing the outcome of the breakup, just that her friend was buggin.

"He moved in with his man. I can't go through this alone anymore. I need you Dolorian and I need Dia and Destini to help me through this shit. I'm scared." Sakina said as she reached for a tissue to dry her face. She started to breakdown right there in front of Dolorian.

"Oh, no, honey. We're about to take care of the problem, so stop your crying. This is a brand new day believe that. I have a plan that I will reveal to you, Dia and Destini tomorrow night at the Cheesecake factory. This is it. Those mother fucking player that screwed us and used us are about to get played. Believe me when I tell you, I have a plan." Dolorian said as she smiled with a big Chester cat smile on her face.

Sakina smiled through the tears. She took Dolorian's hand placing the envelope in it. Dolorain tore it open before Sakina could pull her hand away, pulling out the piece of white paper that Sakina feared touching. Like it was loaded down with the black plague. Dolorian eyes swell as she laid them on the result of the test. "Negative" was splashed across the paper in big black bold letter. She grabbed Sakina's face and showed her the results telling her to pull herself together in order for her to be able to function with a clear head, because they was about to get even. Balancing out the scales of justice on a street level.

"I don't have it!" Sakina yelled to the top of her lungs as she jumped around in her night gown, she had worn for days in a deep dark depression. The results drew a smile to her face through the tears of fear and pain.

"You don't have it baby, see I told you. You were getting all sentimental for nothing," Dolorian said knowing just what to say to comfort her friend Sakina since college. They rolled, way back in the day. Dolorian hated to see a woman cry over something a man inflicted on them. Knowing the games they loved to play with women feelings. She would cut off her right arm to see each one of her friend's men and her own, suffer. And to prove a point she decided to start her little revenge party with K-Killa being the first victim. A plot would be in order.

"I feel a whole lot better now, I'm so glad you called me Dolorian. I don't know what I would do without you in my life, plus Dia and Destini. I need ya'll more than ever since I been on this emotional roller coaster." Sakina said, standing there in her nightgown smelling from days without a shower.

"Listen up, tomorrow night at the Cheesecake factory. Don't forget to dress fly, because afterwards I was thinking we could go down to the men strip club and watch some of those fine ass nigga's sling dick all over the place,. How about it," Dolorian asked as she hugged Sakina to let her know she loved her and would do anything for her.

"Give me those damn pills and a shot of that patron before I go Dolorian knew just what to say out her mouth. She had Sakina mesmerized each time she spoke. She always been straight forward in her approach and Sakina knew this.

"I want you to put those fucked up suicidal thoughts away. Your clean you don't have aids. So now we are going to concentrate on focusing all our energy on fucking Wallace up along with the rest of those no good mother fuckers! They intentionally did this shit to us, Dolorian said before she picked up her prada bag and walked out the door. Sakina leaned against the door knowing when Dolorian said something was going down it was and if she wanted to be down

with making sure Wallace got his just dessert.
She had to straighten up her act.

Dolorian called Dia as to let her know of
the results of the test.

"I just left Sakina and guess what girl her
test came back negative can you believe it? I'm
happy for her she doesn't deserve that shit! That
nigga knew he had a dick pumping him in his ass
and yet he still came home acting like he loved
pussy, I want to plan his demise because he is
not getting away with this shit. Sakina don't
deserve that, why should she have to sit around
her house contemplating suicide while him and
his lover suck each other's big black dicks!"

"Damn, right, girl. That's some fucked up
shit, but I can't be one to talk, after all I thought
my man loved me and look he loves his homeboy
more than he loves me, now what the fuck do you
call that?" Dia said agreeing with everything
Dolorian said out her mouth.

"I don't know." Dolorian said as she
laughed. "But I do know since he love his boys
more than he love you maybe his boy's need to
get fucked up along with him." Dolorain said.

"Yeah, that sounds about right. You better
come tomorrow. I'll be looking for your face in the
place and like I told Sakina dress fly, because
there is no telling where we might end up.
Dolorian said, before she clicks her phone over to
Destini's number.

The continual ring blew her mind. She
hung up ready to try again later.

Dolorian sped through the streets at top
speed. Her BMW truck always attracted attention

and she loved it. The fact that she projected herself as being fly, wearing all the latest babyphat gear she bought online after she seen it on television for the season. Dolorian knew what to do and when to make the right moves. It spoke for itself, she was a trend setter and that is one of the things she thought K-Killa loved about her. As she passed Visions on the way home she noticed a white Yukon Denali like the one K-Killa drove, sitting in the parking lot. She slammed on the breaks sending her beamer into a tail spin. Car blew their horns as her truck slide on the rainy streets before coming to a sudden and complete stop right in front of the club. She stepped out the truck headed for the front door. She hadn't a clue it was a platinum party going on inside for some new recording star, that sold an outrageous amount of records. She just knew K-Killa was in the house and she wanted to know who he had by his side, because as always he had a bitch on his arm. She just knew who ever it was, it sure wasn't his wife. His wifey sat at home aging while he hung out and rode around in all the fines ass cars, his Yukon being just one. His first car he brought was a 1994 Chevrolet Caprice riding on twenty fours, this was the one car Dolorian fell in love with. This was the car K-Killa ate her pussy in, the first time they ever went out on a date. He signed with one of the most prestigious record label in the dirty south and from that point on, the skies been the limit in his recording career. His ego inflated along with his pockets. Where ever he went his entourage led the way. As Dolorian stepped inside, she spotted K-Killa right off the bate with his entourage sitting all around him. The music was loud and the crowd young. Dolorian watched on as Killa handed some honey blonde that look, as if she was under aged a hand full of money. She walked over to the bar to order a drink while Dolorain was observing from the distance. The underage chick walked back over to Killa grinding her body all over his to the music as if he was her man, the music gave her a reason

.

Dolorian saw just about enough. She didn't want to be seen so she slipped out the front door while the party was in full swing. passing by two big black bouncers on the way out.

"I'm going to kill you motherfucker if it's the last thing I do!" Dolorian said with the look of vengeance in her eyes as she twisted her hips harder than ever before heading to her beamer. She had a hard on that made her pussy feel confident. With each step she took it jumped. By the end of the week Marcus. Boo, Wallace and K-Killa would be finished. Somebody would end up in a body bag or in a wheel chair.

She dialed Destini's number one more time before she reached her place of residence.

She knew Destini had a problem with her eyes since Boo set her up to get robbed. Dolorian heard through the grape vine Destini was contemplating going under the knife, like half the women in Georgia, that weren't satisfied with what god gave them.

"Hello?" Destini answered in a soft voice when she finally picked up.

"Lips how are you? I haven't heard from you since we came back from the Caribbean." Dolorian said waiting for Lips to spill her guts. She knew each one of her girl friends was going through something just like she was and the only way to take care of the problem, was bring all questions to the floor and come together creating a clique of revengeful woman.

"I need you to join me and Sakina and Dia tomorrow night at the Cheesecake factory. I have a plan I want to share with ya'll so we can put those nigga to rest. I'm on a mission, girl." Dolorian said

"I know I can hear it in your voice. I was caught up that's why I haven't been in touch. I really been thinking hard about going under the knife. This shit boo did to me really messed me up, Dolorian." Destini said sounding like a broken woman.

"I know. I know." Dolorian said trying to comfort Destini

"I know when we were in the Caribbean I said I would try to let go but it's hard. I've been having a really hard time dating again after Boo. He really broke my spirit." Destini said.

"Don't worry Destini, you know how it is when a woman's fed up? There is nothing a mother fucker can do about it. It's up to us to reclaim our happiness. As you can see, Boo don't care about you, K-Killa don't give a shit about me and poor mentally disturbed Wallace had his wife thinking he left her with a deadly disease and Marcus let his homeboy's rape his woman. So do you really think what we are about to do is wrong?"

CHAPTER 2

"Revenge is a true bitch." Destini said as she snickered.

"Remember what we said before we boarded the plane to come back to the states. We all agreed to this." Dolorian said looking dead serious. "I'm just here to remind ya'll, why should we let sleeping dogs lie. It's time to get retaliation against these dirty bastards! Are you feeling me? Dolorian asked Destini.

"Suppose one of us gets hurt? Trying to get even or even get killed?" I told ya'll when we were in the Caribbean to let the lord handle it, but ya'll want listen to me!" Destini said knowing how devious Dolorian could be when it came to men.

"Snap out of it Destini. Go look in the mirror at your beautiful soft face and look and see how that motherfucker you been letting pump pounds of dick in you every night for years, tried to take away. He took the one and only thing you have." Dolorian said trying to get Destini to see the big picture by proving a point.

"What's that?" Destini asks with suspicion. She hadn't a clue what Dolorian was talking about.

"Your beauty fool! That what he took, can't you see that? Not to mention your mind. You're the one sitting around trying to see if you should go under the knife or not." Dolorian announced as she terminated the call. She left Destini with an ear full before she hung up. Making sure she showed up at the Cheesecake factory for the meeting, to hear the rest of what she had to say. "See you at the Cheesecake factory for dinner."

The hook had been cast and the ladies were all lined up to be at the Cheesecake factory for dinner dressed to impressed. Dolorian made sure of this. The dinner topic would be "revenge is a dish best served cold." Dolorian called to make reservations knowing how hard reservation are to come by and plus she gave lap dances to the owner. She knew just the place to take her girls for a good meal and great conversation, to lift the spirits of the lonely girls. After all, she worked in the entertainment business for years. She knew how to set a mood and how to set a theme. The way her girls sounded on the phone blew her mind, Like Sakina for instance. Sitting around that big empty $1000.00 a month rented house, crying about a test she should have had a long time ago, as soon as she found out from her fag hag lawyer friend. Ayanna Little told her about her man Wallace's love for dick. After he was busted at Atlanta's gay version of visions 708 club, instead of on a plane on the way out of town, like he told his wife he would be. Dia still tried to capture Marcus attention after he called her a "slut". This is after the rape, while on her period that he allowed this to happen to her by his so called friend Rod. Friendship meant more to him then the pussy he laid beside for two years. Destini wanted to go under the knife to bring back something that should have never been taken away from her in the first place, by a nigga she thought worshipped the ground she walked on. Not to mention K-Killa and his slick disappearing acts. He thought money could cure all problems, even the one of a kind fuck he laid on Dolorian, and the fact that his dick was fucking under aged twat now, totally made things worst. The reservations were set and everything in order just like she planned it. Dolorian slung her closet door open looking at all her fabulous outfit from some of the fliest designers. She looked from outfit to outfit until she spotted the right one. The color, fit and style meant a lot on a night like this one. She knew this would be a night with a whole array of surprises in store. The one and only person she knew would help to set things up was a friend of a friend name Peaches. Peaches had her stuff together. Every since her sex change operation, her ass was plumper than that of a woman's and her lips plump like men liked. She paid a pretty penny to be able to fool the naked eye. Her plastic surgeon was like a pimp to her. He got all Peaches money from tricks. She turned on the regular with some high profiled guys. Looking to be on the down low with a pretty fake female face and pussy rooting them on like a cheerleader. Peaches dated lawyer's on the DL, doctors on the DL, Judges on the DL and other guys with secret identities. She was considered bad on the streets by all the other transvestites. When it came to a nip here and a tuck there Peaches was all for it. You could say she was in love with plastic surgery.

She dialed Peaches number.

"Hello?" Dolorian yelled into the phone because where ever Peaches was the music was loud as well as the talking going on in the background.

"Where are you?" Dolorian asks trying to be heard.

"At Bull dogs on Peachtree.

"Hi, honey!" Peaches yelled back.

"Peaches I need you! Dolorian yelled like a woman in distress in the receiver of the phone.

"And why do you need me? If you don't mind me asking?" Peaches said in suspicion.

"It's me Peaches?" Dolorain said identifying herself.

"Me, who?" Peaches ask as she flirted with a male customer who acted as if he needed Peaches services just as bad as Dolorian.

"Money, talks! Bullshit walks! Honey" Peaches said into the receiver.

"I know you know it's me, Dolorian!"

"Oh, honey why you didn't say so. Had me thinking one of my john's wives was calling me, and you know me. I have no time for the wife and kids. Just the dick and my part of the pay check." Peaches said

Dolorian fell out laughing as they talked, before disclosing the real reason for the call.

"I have a big problem on my side of town, Peaches."

"Well, you know Peaches, I'm always happy to assist where assistance is needed." Peaches said. She giggled as she flirts with a trick and held a conversation on her cell phone with Dolorian.

"I need some of that white powder you got for one of the dancers at the club." Dolorian said in a whisper.

"What white powder? What you trying to do sweetie have the DEA all over me?" Peaches said as she laughed.

"I'll bet you'll know exactly what to do for them and to them DEA agents if they were all over you!" Dolorian said before they both laughed.

"Just come by the house I need to talk to you A.S.A.P." Dolorian said trying to talk business.

"Done?" Peaches said before she disconnected.

This made Dolorian's night to hear Peaches voice, and to have her on her side would be all she would be needing. Peaches knew what men wanted and what men needed better than Dolorian, Peaches being a man herself. This is one of the reason Dolorian liked her.

Dolorian pulled out a pair of high heel red Gucci boots. "Beautiful" she said as she slugged them towards her four poster bed. She probed her walk in closets looking for the perfect outfit until she came across one of K-Killa favorites, a little red number he purchased for her in Miami, from one of his wife's favorite boutiques. This made Dolorian frown, but the number was so fly it became irresistible. She slung it on the bed on top of the $880 Gucci boots. This night was to be one to remember and the outfit was just as important. The plot for luring purposes only. Dolorian would never let K-Killa enter her world again no matter how good his dick made her feel. She had morals and principles now and would exercise them to the fullest. She continually day dreamed about all the wild passionate sexual episodes they had on the rebound, until he told her he was married packing up leaving her with a stack of money and a wet pussy. This is what drove her to want to fuck women. She took a deep breath as she walked to one of her three bathrooms to take a bath and spray on her favorite perfume. Dolorian looked in the mirror and wondered how could she had been such a fool, all in the name of good sex Then she thought of one of K-Killa little moves and the way he made her feel when ever they fucked. Her pussy creamed just thinking about it. she loved the fact that he called her baby from time to time leaving her stacks of money and bouncing out on her while he knew shit stank.

Dia finished up the closing deal she worked on through out the day. She wasn't shocked at all by her man's reaction, considering she knew men had a hard time keeping their dicks in their pants. She never thought she would find another man quit like Marcus. She worshipped the ground he walked on rather than visa versa. Even after the rape she wanted him back. She would learn to be cool with him having other honeys on the side if that's what he wanted. This is the thought that ran through her head while she day dreamt. Sitting at her desk thinking about the purpose of this whole dinner Dolorian was throwing together, trying to start some static taking revenge on the enemy this was like the revolution in Dia's eyes and her job came first, after all she had to pay the bills and wouldn't want to get her hands dirty. She came along way since the violation committed against her in Rod's basement. But since she promised Dolorian she'd be there she decided to go and show some support for Sakina and her mental triumph over the disease aids and the unmoral break up of her and her husband Wallace.

"What should I wear? Dia, thought to herself before one of her colleagues peeped in to say goodnight before leaving the office.

Dia closed the file cabinet and locked it. She picked up her Metallic gold Gucci purse and jacket to match putting it on her beautiful strong frame. Her large eyes scanned the room to assure her she wasn't leaving anything behind that she would need before the night was out. She walked out locking the door to her office behind her. Headed to her red Audi ragtop parked curbside the door of the real-estate office. She got in the car and called Dolorian letting her know she would meet her at the cheesecake factory, but she would be a little late.

Sakina's phone rang.

"I hope you're getting dressed. We're taking my car tonight. I'll be by to pick you up in an hour so, be ready." Dolorian announced as she sipped on her glass of Monet. A celebration was taking place right there in her bed room knowing she had all the ponds in order and the games would begin.

"Like playing a game of chess." Dolorian said to herself as she slipped on her skin tight red Gucci jeans with the g's all over them to match her boots and jacket and hat that set the whole outfit off. She was on fire and her outfit told the story.

"Fuck you K-Killa. I can pull any of these men in the ATL I want, to including women. You knew this, but yet you're out here taking my love for granted. I'll show you who the Bella mafia in this fucked up family, and it sure ain't your wife." Dolorian said as she sprayed another round of First perfume, by van Cleef & Arpel on her neck, wrist and cleavage. The places that men and woman loved to put their noses. She knew there was going to be a lot of questions to answer at this meeting that she put together from scratch, and none of her girls would be willing to put their careers on the line to bring a couple of no good ass nigga's down to their knees. Their careers paid the house bills, the car notes, the grocery bill, not to mention the light, gas, and cable bill, and the bill to have a little fun every now and then.

Dolorian knew Peaches would be dropping by before she left to go to the Cheesecake factory. Just as she cut out the lights in her bedroom and closed the door the doorbell rang. Dolorian looked at herself in the long floor length mirror before going down stairs to let Peaches in. She peeped out the side of the blinds and seen a long stretch limo in the front yard with a chauffer standing there ready to served, if asked too.

"Look at this bitch!" Dolorian said beforc opening her front door.

Peaches gown was so long and tight she needed the chauffer to carry the tail of it up to the front door.

"Peaches!" Dolorian screamed as she grabbed her to hug.

"Watch the gown sweetie! This is an Allen Schwartz original." Peaches said as she walked in the door switching harder than any woman.

"I was hoping you would come and as usually you look gorges."

Dolorian said as she stepped to the side letting Peaches in.

"You look kind of hot yourself. Turn around and let Peaches see what you working with!" Peaches held her arms out as Dolorian spun around.

Dolorian did a three sixty revealing her goodies in there true form.

"Come over here and have a seat darling. I'm sorry I called on such short notice." Dolorian said

"I don't have time for all of that. I left my date in the car. He's taking me ballroom dancing with the stars. Can't you just see it, him with his face in my crouch during the whole dance?" Peaches said as she peeped out the blinds making sure the limo was still there. She knew how men were phoned for changing their minds with the quickness.

Now, what's the distress? When you called me I thought you were over here getting your ass whipped. Now where's the problem? That you wanted this white powder for." Peaches ask as she looked around the room as if she missed something.

"The problem doesn't live here any more. So there is no reason to look around." Dolorian expressed.

"Well, where in the fuck is he!" Peaches said all hyped up.

"Calm down Peaches."

"No, you ask me about white powder on the phone. I feel like I'm being set up!" Peaches said looking dead serious and paranoid.

"Hell no, girl, I have a problem with my man, Dia's man, and Sakina's husband, and Destini's man are all absconders and we want to get even for all the heartache and pain they caused us. That's why I called you to ask for some of that white powder. I have a plan that includes that same white powder you gave to one of the dancer's at the club a couple of years back."

"Oh, you're talking about the gamma," Peaches said. She couldn't wait to analyze this problem Dolorian was talking about.

"What's the name?" Dolorian asked she just knew what the outcome of the dancer's problem was after she gave her man some of the gamma she bought from Peaches. One night she was hoping to put her man to sleep because every night he would whipped her ass, when she came home from work. The gamma put him to sleep permanently. The dumb bitch gave her man an overdose."

"If that's what you gave the dancer. That's the same thing I want." Dolorian said.

"Woo...slow down sweetie. That stuff is dangerous. Are you sure that's how you want to handle this situation?" Peaches asked, knowing how love could make a woman do crazy things. She also knew the outcome of giving the dancer the gamma. She was arrested and did a ten year bid after the fact for first degree murder with intent.

"I tell you what. I didn't bring it with me but you can meet me at the club tomorrow evening and I'll give you all the gamma you want. But I'm going to tell you like I told the dancer, use it sparingly." Peaches terminated the conversation before her rich dick left her clear on the other side of Georgia. Peaches took hold of the tail of her Allen Swartz gown and tipped toed to the limo, slipping on a pair of silk gloves to cover her big hands on the way.

When A Woman's Fed Up

CHAPTER 3

Dolorian's outfit didn't say nothing compared to Sakina's when she stepped out her front door dressed to impressed. Like commanded to by Dolorian. She represented Jimmy Choo to the fullest extent. Her hair was fly as well as the Jimmy Choo shoes. Satin d' Orsay Pumps she wore as Sakina walked proudly to Dolorian's car, switching like it was a brand new day and no one could defer her progress. This did Dolorian's heart glad to see her friends spirits lifted in such a short period of time.

"You look very elegant if I must say so myself." Dolorian said as Sakina plopped her hips on the red leather interior.

"I feel sexy." Sakina responded.

"I know you do. And I know after tonight all those crazy thoughts of suicide will not be in you life anymore, am I right?" Dolorian assuring Sakina she had her back.

"What's this plan you're talking about anyway?" Sakina asks with deep suspicion.

"I'm not telling. After I pick everybody up, I will be making a little announcement that can't be revealed at dinner.

Dolorian pulled up to Destini's house and blew the horn the door opened almost immediately. Destini spirits were down. You could see it pass the dark Christian Dior shades she sported, to match her designer slip dress with a pair of good shoes and a bag to match.

"You go girl!" Sakina yelled out the window as she watched her come closer to the car with sparkles in her eyes.

Destini smiled she needed Dolorian, Sakina, and Dia to pull her out the dumps more than ever.

"Why aren't you smiling? Shit, you' are supposed to be happy, girl!' Dolorian asked, knowing she was laughing and talking on the phone with her just moments earlier.

"I'm not happy worth a motherfuck. That's why I'm not smiling. Like you said earlier on the phone he took everything I had, look at me! I'm so embarrassed at the way my eye looks I'm scared to be seen in public without dark shades on to cover the scares."

Destini started to tear up. Sakina turned around in her seat to show her she was there for her.

"If you go under the knife we'll be there for you." Sakina said as she grabbed her friend's hand showing her support.

"I love ya'll." Destini said as she dried her eyes before her mascara ran all over her five hundred dollar Christian Dior dress.

"We love you back. Dia will be meeting us at the Cheesecake factory she told me she'd be a little late. Dolorian announced.

"What's the plan then, I have to know before we get to the restaurant." Destini asked and Sakina wanted to know just as bad. All eyes shifted in Dolorian's direction.

"Well, I guess I can share this much with ya'll. A friend of mine is getting me a little bit of gamma. And I'm going to give it to K-Killa and make him beg for mercy, for the shit he did to me. If this is the same kind of revenge you want to take out on your man then I will get enough to satisfy all. If not, we will find another way to deal with Wallace, Marcus and Boo." Dolorian said. Everybody in the car was silent like obedient school aged girls. They knew when Dolorian talked, especially about men, there was no interrupting. A master of the subject, everybody else was like pupils being taught a lesson.

"I don't know what I want to do to Wallace yet. He already has the aids, what else is there I could do to him, after all the man's dying." The car became silent again as the brain behind the operation took the floor.

"Make that motherfucker beg, that's what you can do to him. Fuck him having aids, he brought that sentence upon himself, by disrespecting his wife. All you did was tried to be a good wife to that faggot and this is the thanks you get. Fuck that! Believe me we're going to save the best nigga's for last and that being Wallace."

Sakina eyes got real big as Dolorian's mouth continued to move, and all the stuff that came out of it were all pertaining too revenge, vendetta, vengeance, retaliation and justice. An eye for an eye and a tooth for a tooth. The speech continued until they drove up to the Cheesecake factory where cheesecake came at 5,000 calories a slice in a wide variety of flavors. The food there is displayed artfully. Dolorian knew this was the place to be under a cozy setting.

"The food is out of this world here, girls!" Sakina said as she watched on as Dolorian looked for a parking spot.

"They have valet parking, girls."

"Fuck a valet. I can park my own shit! This bitch is always crowded, that what I hate about it." Dolorian said as she maneuvered her car in a backwards mode, backing up into a parking space on the street across from the restaurant.

"Fuck the wait! The food is worth it and the raspberry martinis are to die for." Destini popped out from under her hypnotic state and participated in the conversation. As the ladies exited the car walking up to the restaurant with the crowd of pedestrians looking flier than word could express. Men were dead on it. As they watched this beautiful trio walk right in. passing all the other customers, and be seated before all the people in line, that had been standing there for an hour or more.

"How in the hell did you manage to get in pass everybody else? Sakina whispered in Dolorian's ear as she felt special walking up to the table.

"I use to give the owner lap dances at the club. He would always come all over himself before I could finish, every time like clock work."

"Oh." Sakina answered, not stunned by the answer, as she strutted to her seat.

The hostess took the three ladies out to the patio where lights filled the trees and a beautifully lit fountain displayed water works of color were in affect. The ladies ordered drinks

"I'll have a raspberry martini, bake chicken and cranberry sauce." Destini ordered, knowing the menu backwards and forwards from pass date here with her man.

Sakina and Dolorian looked at her with surprise.

"You know what you want right off the back don't you?" Dolorian asks.

"Boo and I use to come here all the time." Destini said as she looked around the room searching for a familiar face in the crowd.

"I'll have a Caesars salad with a side of that delicious Italian ziti. Light on the parmesan please" Dolorian said.

"I don't know what I want yet just come back to me." Sakina said as she searched the sixteen page menu. Excited to be liberated out of the prison she'd been in ever since her husband walked out on her. Loading up his vehicle with all his valuables. Driving off never once looking back.

"I'm glad all my girls made it except one." Dolorian said as she looked at her Gucci watch. Just as she did, Dia walked up wearing an egg shell white number, from Dolce and Gabbana outfits, revealing lots of brown skin.

"I was hoping you would make it!" Dolorian said checking her out from head to toe as she sat down beside her.

"I wouldn't miss this for the world, especially if you got a plan." Dia said as she picked up her menu and looking it over.

"Like I told the ladies in the car. I have a friend who is getting me a supply of gamma." Dolorian whispered in Dia's ear not wanting the whole restaurant to hear what was on her mind.

"Gamma, who are you trying to put to sleep?" Dia asked, not looking surprised. She just knew who ever was getting some gamma was about to get some real shit done to them.

"What you know about gamma? Dia," and Dolorian wanting to hear, how wise Dia claimed to be about pharmaceuticals. She waited patiently to see what she was going to reveal.

Before you tell me wait a minute, Bartender! Can you please bring me a drink?" Dolorian asked, with a loud voice turning heads. The waitress quickly ran over to their patio table and took the ladies order.

"Bring us a round of Remy and my friend Sakina's favorite, Patron." Dolorian said, making Sakina laugh. Sakina knew Dolorian was the only one, out of all the ladies sitting at the table who knew her secret thoughts of suicide, because Dolorian seen her suicide kit sitting on the table in her living room while she held on to the aids test, anticipating the answer. This is the thought that ran through Sakina's mind while Dolorian ordered a round of drinks.

The waitress ran off to get the orders, while the ladies continued the conversation where they left off.

"Now, what is it you said you know about gamma? Dia" Dolorian presumed.

"I know guys in a sorority in the college I went too that used gamma on girls they wanted to fuck. They would invite them to parties and slip it in their drinks. It supposes to turn blue when they put it into someone's drink." Dia explained.

The man sitting in the seat beside them turned around and looked at Dolorian with a smirk on his face.

"Is there something over here you want?' Dolorian asks.

He turned back around minding his business.

The ladies sat closer and whispered this time, when they talked.

"I knew this one girl, the same sorority members used it on. She died. The poor girl vomited her guts out, at least it seemed like she did. When I saw her, her plus she was anorexic. That was some scary shit too. I was young, so of course I was scared. She was hallucinating they said, through the campus grapevine when the guys took it."

"Took what?" Sakina asks.

"Took her pussy and asshole before they killed her with the gamma!" Dia said loud enough for half the restaurant to hear. The man next to their table held his drink up to the ladies and they all laughed.

"I told you I seen K-Killa at a platinum party and hugged up on some body's baby. He's fuckin babies now." Dolorian said as all the ladies shook their heads to her accusations about her man. She looked hurt when she said it, getting a lump in her throat.

"Damn, girl, I know you wanted to shake him on the spot, huh?" Destini asks.

"Damn right I wanted to kill him on the spot, but what could I do he's married and plus he never really loved me anyway. I feel sorry for his wife. I'm going to bust that motherfuckers bubble once and for all." Dolorian said trying to sound hard.

"Yeah, I still love Marcus too." Dia said under her breath. The restaurant wasn't helping the situation. A familiar place in the history in her mind brought back memories where she and Marcus hung out on numerous occasions.

"I would have never fucked his friends if he would have just told me not too, he insisted. Why would he tell me to fuck him and then disc me afterwards, that's the problem. He really hurt me ya'll!" Dia said ringing her alarm in the air into the ears of the pedestrians at surrounding tables.

The conversation got red hot like Dolorian's outfit and the plans were being set in motion.

"Number one ladies we will not be getting our hands dirty. Number two I'm calling K-Killa wife once and for all. I let this ride for far too long now and I hate to see her be his fool like I was. And your man Destini, I plan on hiring somebody to fuck him up, believe me that's already in the makings. His hangout is Peppers bar and grill on Friday night. I seen him and his boy's hugged up on an entourage of south side ho's, but they didn't see me. I dodged out the back door." Dolorian explained, as she made all kinds of hand gestures.

As she talked, Sakina soft heart penetrated her thoughts. She thought about how Wallace was a smart, handsome, hardworking man and an affectionate lover from time to time. He'd been an old fashion provider for her, ever since she could remember, and now it all boiled down to this. She hadn't a clue what she wanted to do to him as far as vigilantism, because that wasn't her department. But if Dolorian, Dia and Destini came up with something she wasn't about to wimp out. Then her devilish thoughts took over, she thought about how he lied about being out of town and the fact that he became disenchanted with Sakina. This drove her wild inside, just thinking about it. She would be down for what ever at this point and the risk factor involved was little to nothing. No gamble would be involved. Since Dolorian claimed, neither one of the ladies had to get their hands dirty. All she had to do was sit back and watch this horrid punishment of a whipped nigga like Wallace. She laughed to herself.

"What ever ya'll come up with I'm down!" Sakina yelled as she put her glass of Remy up to her plump lips. All could see the liquors effects were being felt. Each and everybody at this table were feeling right. The atmosphere in the restaurant became serene.

"And as for Marcus I laid there half the night to think up this one, check it out. I want him to get a taste of his own medicine since he didn't care about you the night he let his boy's stick dick all up in your ass." Dolorian said. The man at the next table finished his meal and walked over to the table where the ladies sat.

"Thank you for making my lonely dinner interesting." Dolorian, Sakina, Dia and Destini laughed. The man walked out off the patio. Dolorian resumed her conversation; she explained the strategy of the whole plan to the girls. She didn't want to leave no stones up turned.

"Marcus, Marcus, Marcus. I want him to get raped just like he let you get raped." Dolorian said. All the girls' mouths hung open.

"How in the hell are we going to manage that?" Dia asks

"Yeah." Sakina asks agreeing with Dia.

Destini laughed as some of her liquor rolled down her cheek. The statement Dolorian made was funny.

"I have someone I'm going to pay to fuck him and his boy Rod in the asshole. What do ya'll have to say about that?" Dolorian asks as she stood up holding her glass in one hand and the other on her hip.

"A man getting raped! That's some Devious shit" Dia said, feeling quit tipsy.

"Yes, honey, it happens everyday. It don't matter how big the nigga is, there's always somebody bigger, it don't matter how strong that nigga, is there's always somebody stronger.

With a drink in her hand, Dia laughed at every word that came out of Dolorian's mouth. Stronger honey, Male rape can happen at home, work, even in the fucking bathroom at the club." Dolorian fell out laughing. Along with each one of her girls the plan she had in effect was working, each word that came out her mouth was agreed upon just like she wanted. Sakina had a smile on her. Destini was shocked to think a man could get raped. This she would have to see with her own two eyes.

"He had you gangbanged baby. Pay back is and will be a bitch just watch and see what I say."

"Your talking that eye for an eye a tooth for a tooth stuff girl, I'm scared of you." Destini said.

"I don't want to hurt the man I laid with, given pussy too every night for years. But this is what it all boils down too." Dolorian explained.

Each person put their hands on the table making a pact. They wouldn't quit until the job was done, even if it hurt to see it happened.

CHAPTER 4

The girls could had voted on burning down a house or even for one of the men that did them wrong to get stabbed down in the streets like they deserved. Dia knew if she would have reported the rape to the authorities none of this would probably be happening.

"How about that old cliché, when people use to say that the only way to a man's heart is through his stomach?" Destini said turning everybody at the table heads in her direction. "I know your not talking about poisoning no body?" Sakina asked with suspicion.

"So what do you call using gamma? That's a form of poising, whether you know it or not." Destini said, as she held her drink extra tight in her hand. "Shit, if your going to do that shit, at least you could do the shit right." Destini expressed before turning the glass up to her mouth gulping down the remainder of her Remy. The conversation was getting heated as the conversation about revenge flowed like water.

Dolorian looked at Destini rolling her eyes.

"All I have to say is as far as tomorrow night goes is. I need each one of you ladies to meet me at my house by ten o'clock no later then that please. So we can plan this shit right. All in all we're going to have to lure these motherfucker's to a destination, where we can do what we want to do to them. As far as tonight goes we 're taking back our dignity, respect and love for self and all the good shit we should be feeling about ourselves, because a motherfucker wanted to stick his dick in another ho. Why should we suffer, but in your case Sakina another man." Dolorian said, as she took control of the whole floor plan once again.

"How in the hell am I supposed to lure Wallace ass back to the house?" Sakina asked.

"You're not going to lure him to the house. You're going to lure him to the hotel Twelve, and once there, it will be out of your hands. Do you understand that Sakina? I will have the people lined up, who are being paid to carry out the plan. They will take over from there. It's up to you, if you want to stick around and watch what ever floats your boat. That will have to be your own choice." Dolorian explained knowing she was the one who was co-creating the whole plan.

"So how in the hell do women lure a gay man to a hotel room? Isn't that another gay man's job" Sakina asks with curiosity in her voice. The ladies at the table fell out with laughter.

"Shit, at gun point! He might get shot before his ass get to the room, if I have something to do with it!" Dia said as she opened her purse showing her girlfriends the weapon she had purchased down the block at a pawn shop. Dia agreeing with everything Dolorian said.

"Who are you planning on using that on?" Sakina asks, as her eyes practically bucked out her head. She had a phobia about guns.

"I wanted to kill that motherfucker, I called my man!" Dia said, I actually sat outside his job one evening waiting for him to come out. Luckily he didn't show up that day. I was going to shoot that motherfucker! You just don't know." Dia expressed.

"I know you don't want to go down like that and end up in the women's penitentiary, honey." Dolorian said. "Just let me handle this shit." Dolorian said as she put her hands up stopping all conversation flow.

"Yeah, I know you'll know what to do, Dolorian, after all, nobody know men like you do!" Sakina said trying to win Brownie point with her long time friend.

"I have a couple of men I know who would do what ever I want them to, for some pussy!" Dolorian said, and one of them just so happen to be mob associated" Dolorian announced.

"I never knew you knew anybody in mob?" Sakina said.

"Everything is not to be announced. All you need to know is, there are a time and a place for everything." Dolorian explained, as she built up a boost of confidence with the information about the men she knew who were mob associated.

"Are you talking about the black mob or the Italian mafia?"

"No, I'm talking about street thug mafia." Dolorian said

"These nigga's got their shit tight too; believe me when I tell you." Dolorian explained as she finished her drink and stood up.

"So do these thugs know who our ex-men are already?" Sakina asks.

"Hell no! First and fore most, I want to do my man before I do anybody else's lost dicks. K-Killa's black ass will be the first domino to fall flat on his face starting tonight. I have a very important phone call to make; his wife is the first target. I want that bitch to hurt just like I'm hurting." Dolorian felt the affects of her drink and the ladies that looked up to her could see she was drunk .it was time to go home after all she was the one driving.

"I don't think that would be such a good idea not tonight anyway Dolorian. Look at you your drunk; I guess that cancels the club; huh." Sakina said, looking around at each one of her girl's friend's faces, to see their expressions.

"Fuck the club. I just want to kill something." Dolorian said, as she turned around headed to the ladies room stumbling down the isle on the way.

The next day Dolorian slept straight through the whole day. She awoke with a killer hangover and K-Killa on the brain. She picked up the crystal clock that sat on her vanity table beside her bed noticing the big hand on the eight and the little hand on the twelve. She jumped out of bed holding her head in the palm of her hands. The meeting at Bulldogs was to be this night and

Peaches promised her all the gamma she wanted, with the promise of her using it sparingly, because the drug could kill if not used right.

"Shit, ain't this a bitch, I'm late." Dolorian showered and slipped on a black outfit to match her mood with the black hat and dark glasses to cover up her swollen red eyes. No hangover was worth not meeting with Peaches. She drove through the streets with fire in her heart and a script in her head. The words played over and over like a broken record of the Conversation she would have with K-Killa's wife. She wanted K-Killa, for making her fall in love with him. Undercover, but little did she know he wouldn't have cared, because love was nothing to a man like him, only music, groupies giving away free pussy, and his entourage that made him look good when ever he pulled up in a driveway at a club. The only thing that really meant anything of value to K-Killa was the recording contract he signed with his blood sweat and tears. Dolorian should have known pussy didn't rule him like woman thought it could.

Even a woman like Dolorian, even thought she knew everything about a man. She really didn't, and the fact was because she could even keep her own man. She lived a lie with him for far too long and the only way to release the pressure on her heart that love created, was to kill, leaving no victim alive to talk about it. She knew Peaches told her too much about gamma could kill. Dolorian's demons rose up in the pit of her stomach, telling her to give K-Killa. All the gamma she was about to collect from Peaches and she planned to do just that.

Sakina walked around her big empty house wondering could and would she ever find love again. She was getting a whole lot older and young girls seemed to be in. Even thought Wallace left her for a man. Her heart still went out to him. She knew he had to be scared and crushed to know that the disease that kills so many had finally come knocking at his door. She put her arms around herself before picking up the phone to call Dolorian.

"Hi, Dolorian I need to see you." Sakina said in a sad voice.

"Oh, shit I know you're not over there bugging out again. Didn't we talk about this last night? Everything is in the makings, so just sit back and let me do my work!" Dolorian hung up the phone, for she was on a mission speeding thought the streets like a crazy woman. She couldn't afford to let Peach ride off with one of her tricks. She knew men loved what ever it was Peaches did to them and would give Peaches what ever she wanted. From Jewels, to fur coats, nice cars one of her tricks went as far as to set Peaches up in a Condo overlooking the city of Atlanta. So he could sneak over and fuck her in the ass when ever the feeling hit him.

Dolorian knew she was down with the in crowd and she was willing to go where ever the in crowd went. She pulled up to Bulldogs. The neon light shined in her eyes as she searched for a parking space. It was obvious a party was in affect. Dolorian went to pull in a parking space as a big Black Hummer truck pulled up in front of her. She stepped out of her vehicle cussing ready to fight over a parking space.

"Excuse me bitch, I was here first." A transvestite said, as her and her girl friends, cross dressers stepped down on to the pavement wearing pumps. The woman was so tall Dolorian quickly got back in her car searching for an alternative parking space. She knew if she would have thrown the first punch it would have turned into a full blown riot, with faggots popping up from out of no where, ready to kick ass and take names. She imagined what she would see when she opened the bar door. The house was packed, she could have sworn that every sexually twisted creator on gods green earth was in the house dancing and partying like it was the end of the world. Rogue Paul was being played on the turn tables by a DJ wearing lips stick and big gold earring. Dolorian chuckled to herself as she walked through the crowd of designer outfits, made for a woman but worn by men. Only to find a long stretched out table with human bodies laid upon it. The models that participated in this table topper were all decorated as human food.

"This shit is unreal." Dolorian said as she started to ask any and everybody where Peaches was.

"Excuse me have you seen Peaches here tonight?" She asked all and every Trans in her path.

"Who are you? I don't know you, so why would I tell you where Peaches is?" the Trans asked as she held onto a leech with some body's husband on the end of it. She hit him with a whip. Her submissive wore a collar like an animal, while the Trans gave all the orders. You could tell she was a dominatrix by calling, she did her job well She made her submissive get down on the floor and lick her toes while she talk to Dolorian. Dolorian laughed. She had seen just about enough. This party was way out of control and Peaches face was no where in the crowd. She continued to walk, until she walked over to the bar asking the bartender for Peaches.

"She's in the bathroom in my office do you want to talk to her or something?" The bartender asked as he pushed a drink in Dolorian direction.

"No..." Dolorian said

"This is on the house baby." The bartender said, as he tried to give her the drink once again.

"I couldn't drink that if I tried. I'm still hungover from last night. You said Peaches is in the bathroom in your office. Well would it be alright if I go back there, because I'm supposed to meet her here tonight." Dolorian explained to the bartender.

"Yeah go on back." The bartender opens his office door letting Dolorian in. As she closed the door behind her she could hear slight moans as if someone was hurt.

"Peaches are you in there?" Dolorian tapped on the bathroom door waiting to get an answer.

"Oh..." The voice in the bathroom moaned out once again the noise became louder and louder. Until Dolorian's suspicion wouldn't let her walk away without knowing who was behind the closed door with Peaches and what ungodly activities was going on. She turned the door knob pushing the door all the way open to find Peaches with her trick in the john fucking. Peaches was bent over with her fly designer dress hyped up not caring who seen her. The trick was so excited he continued to fuck not caring that the door to the bathroom revealed his identity.

"I'm here waiting for you Peaches." Dolorian said in a soft voice before backing out of the door frame.

"Can't you see I'm fucking?" Peaches yelled as her trick continually made her jump with each thrust.

"I'll being waiting for you at the bar." Dolorian said as she walked back out into the twisted party that was taking place, taking a seat at the bar.

Peaches walked out of the office holding her purse in one hand while fixing her weave with the other.

"I got it for you. I'm fully aware of the reason you're here so there is no need to ask me for what you want once again." Peaches said as she reached in her purse and slipped a white envelope with twenty tablets of gamma in it.

"I'm going to tell you once again, use it sparingly. And remember you didn't get this from me." Peaches said as she winked and turned around walking into the mitts of the party.

CHAPTER 5

Dolorian rode down the highway headed back home her girls were to meet her there at ten sharp as she ordered, when they plotted and planned at the Cheesecake factory. She wondered could she really pull it off. All kinds of doubts played in her head all of a sudden. The confidence she had built up from being driven to a point of murder was slipping away. She put her ear piece on while at a stop light, after exiting the highway. She Dialed K-Killa's wife phone number hoping she would pick up the phone, she didn't. The phone rang until an answering machine come on. The voice that blurted out of it made her even madder. The message on the machine had been recorded by K-Killa and his wife together. Their voices rung out in her ear, creating more madness. To top off the already fucked up situation even worst.

"I know you don't know me but I have a few things to say to you about your man/husband. I've been fucking him for two years now and he'd even stayed with me while in town. His career is making him into a total and complete monster. He used me and I thought you should know he's not as loyal as he claimed to be. If you want to know more call me at. 404-223-3131, and I'll give you an ear full when you call."

Dolorian switched over to a dial tone. She took a deep breath, knowing something was coming out of the message she had just left on K-Killa's wife machine.

She wouldn't stop at just K-Killa's wife. She had to line up the plans for Wallace to be lured to Hotel Twelve, only after she convinced K-Killa she needed to see him. The Hotel twelve services wouldn't be need for K-Killa. She wanted him in her bed one last time before she snuffed his life out. Dolorian decided to give K-Killa an overdose of gamma. She planned on calling him to set everything up.

She dialed his number.

"Hello." Killa answered, sounding kind of down.

"K it's me Dolorian."

"Hi baby I'm glad you called. I need you." K said into the receiver melting Dolorian's pussy as usual, making her melt all over the place.

"Do you miss me like I miss making love to you?' K asked. All became silent.

"I just called to find out if we could meet. Is it at all possible you could swing by my place tonight?' Dolorian asked waiting for K's answer.

"That could be arranged, I'll bring a bottle of champagne to celebrate us getting back together. What do you have to say about that?' K asked

"Ok." Dolorian said forgetting she had a pocket book full of gamma to fuck K-Killa up, just as quickly as he said hello. She thought back to the last time they were together. Then the thought of the teenager hanging from his arm at Visions, resurrected the plans. Bringing them back to life like they where supposed to be.

"I'll be there around twelve is that alright?" K asked, before he disconnected.

"Twelve it is." Dolorian said as she hanged up.

She pulled into her driveway and sat there before going inside the house. She had a change in her plans with the girls tonight. She never imagined calling K-Killa to spend the night with her so she could take him down first. Things were falling right into place like they should have been. She smiled to herself feeling confident that since he was coming and no one knew he was coming she would be able to give him an overdose of gamma, and watch him beg for mercy, while stretched out in the floor. She would become a murder before the night was out. She phoned Sakina, Dia and Destini to let them know she would see them the following day because something came up. She didn't want to reveal that she had the gamma, because she knew once she started crushing pills, preparing them to go inside of the champagne K-Killa was bringing for the get back together celebration. His celebration would turn into a funeral, little did he know.

Dolorian called Sakina first.

"Sakina I have to cancel our plans for tonight. I know I told you girls to meet me over at my place at ten, but something's come up. So tomorrow morning will be sufficient." Dolorian explained.

"Are you alright, Dolorian?' Sakina asked with a concerned voice.

"Everything's fine, I just feel a little under the weather that's all." Dolorian said.

"Can you call the others for me Sakina and let them know tomorrow morning I will call each one of ya'll to meet me at Hotel Twelve, so we can get a room for the festivities to begin."

"I just hope what we are about to do won't get none of us locked up. We have too much to lose for that to happen. Ain't no man worth all that." Sakina said making complete sense. Dolorian listened but not hearing what Sakina was saying.

"See you tomorrow," Dolorian said as she hanged up the phone. She opened the front door to her house and walked into the thick blackness of the dark. Lingerie would have to be a part of what she wanted to create with K-Killa tonight. Something that she never really took the time to do. Se would have to know as soon as he walked into her domain that shit had changed and he wouldn't be getting her back 100% like he hoped.

She ran straight to her lingerie draw and looked through all the Victoria Secret lingerie she had bought, but never used. She knew K-Killa wasn't interested in lingerie like that. She could be wearing a potato shack dress and he would still want to fuck her. She pulled out a turquoise number, holding it up to the light to see if her body parts would be revealed in it like she wanted them to be exposed. The light would tell the story. She would play the game of illusionist tonight, mastering all kinds of illusions just to get the gamma where it needed to be in K-Killa's drink. Just as she laid her FX, that would bring with it special effects out on the bed, the phone rung.

"Hello." She answered extremely quick, not aware it was K-Killa wife on the phone.

"Hello?" Kelly said in a soft innocent young voice.

"Hi. Whom am I talking with?' Dolorian asked as she sat on the edge of the bed, wondering if it was K-Killa wife's voice on the other end.

"I received a message on my answering machine telling me my husband is unfaithful?" The young voice asked.

Dolorian became silent for a minute. She couldn't believe K-Killa wife was so young. She knew he loved young girls from seeing him at the club snuggled up with one. She begins to tell her the reason for the call.

"Hi, I'm Dolorian and yes I left the message. Your husband is K-Killa am I right?" Dolorian asked, ready to play mind games.

"My name is Kelly and yes K is my husband. On my answering machine you said he slept with you?"

All became silent once again.

"Yes he slept with me and I just wanted you to know. I said to myself. Self, K-Killa's wife needs to know he's cheating not just with me, but with a whole bunch of young girls here in

Atlanta, Georgia. He slings more dick then Elvis."
Dolorian said.

"Well, Dolorian, I'm well aware of my
husband sex addiction. We even tried going to
counseling, nothing seems to work for him. So all
I can do is be a good wife and support him in
what ever decision he decides to make." Kelly
explained, knowing Dolorian wasn't telling her
nothing she wasn't aware of.

"Damn," Dolorian said, not knowing K-Killa
was a sex addict. She knew he knew how to lay
his pipe. She had been fucking him for two years
and never was the wiser that he attended
counseling sessions.

"Well is that all you wanted to tell me?
Dolorian"

"Yes I just wanted to tell you that and that
I'm fucking him tonight." Dolorian said before she
throws her cell phone across the room, it landed
on her bed. She wasn't about to give Kelly her
address. So she just acted as if the information
she had just received about K-Killa's sex
addiction didn't penetrate her being along, with
her ears. She had to get ready; K would be
knocking on the door in a matter of minutes. The
house had to look just right and her body had
smell of fresh flowers to turn him on like she
wanted to. After she stepped out the hot
steaming bath, she put on the turquoise lingerie.
She sat down on the couch, but not before
putting on some soft jazz to set the mood. She
grabbed for her purse pulling out the gamma
pills. She placed each one in a white hankie, she
had in her hands. She picked up a big crystal

rock that she sat in the middle of the living room table as decoration. She folded the hankie and then crushed the pilled. As she did, a blue smoky substance polluted her space. She was inhaling the mist that she breathed into her lungs. Dolorian sneezed. There was a mellow knock at the front door.

"Coming." Dolorian yelled over Kenny G saxophone

She opened the door and stepped to the side, letting K-Killa in. Revealing her sexy lingerie.

"Hay baby." K said before he picked her up and swung her around showing how much he really missed her.

I know you know I missed you?" Dolorian said, trying to gain her ex-man's confidence.

"I love the lingerie, so is this supposed to be the new you?" K asked as he handed her the bottle of Monet.

"I guess you could call it that." Dolorian answered.

"I knew exactly what to buy when I walked in the liquor store. This is a night of many nights to come. I will be spending a lot more time with you. I came to that conclusion when I spotted you creeping out the door at Visions. I know you didn't think I saw you but I did, and I know when you seen who I was with, it hurt you, and I want to apologize for hurting you so much during our relationship," K-Killa said, as he plopped down on the sofa. He talked like he was talking to a shrink. Dolorian couldn't believe it. Dolorian was at a lost for words, was this the K-Killa she seen with the teenager at Visions or had some aliens caught up with him and his entourage and snatched bodies. She felt guilty for a minute before the picture of her and her girls at the Cheesecake factory came into view

She remembered the drunken pact they all made, to never give up until the job of getting revenge was done and she planned on doing just that.

"Let me go get us some wine glasses" Dolorian said, as she hoped the pills she had just crushed would dissolve before she returned to the living room where K-Killa sat.

CHAPTER 6

Dolorian opened the hankie and poured the gamma into the wine glass. She looked up and asked for forgiveness in a silent tongue before doing so. Her heart was worth more than the lie and dream K-Killa was about to sell her, like he was a dream merchant. She wasn't buying this time.

"What are you doing in there? Hurry up so I can hold you in my arms." K-Killa yelled through Dolorain's house, as he sat there with his legs stretched out like he was at home. She closed her eyes and took a deep breath before proceeding to walk back into the front room with the turquoise furry slippers on, to match her lingerie. She switched her behind in K-Killa's face, drawing his attention from the wine glasses to her ass. She handed K-Killa the glass, his smile brought back a lot of old memories, but this was more important considering. She knew a man's word was all he had and if he didn't have that, the man was nothing and if K-Killa couldn't be man enough to tell her he had a sex addiction problem, and then he sure wouldn't confess his sins now. Dolorian knew his intentions were to fuck her and leave her like he did so many times before, then run off into the arms of another. She would prevent that shit from happening this time.

K-Killa took a sip of his champagne, as Dolorian turned her glass up to her plump lips while looking at him from the corner of her eye as he drank the gamma. She knew it would be a matter of minutes before he felt its effects.

"Come on let's go into the bedroom," She said, as she grabbed his hand leading him on as if she was glad to see him.

K-Killa gulped down the remainder of his drink and asked for another one as a chaser.

"You're mighty thirsty tonight baby. I haven't spent time with you in a long time and when you come around you just want to drink, what's up with that?" Dolorian said, trying to make him feel guilty for leaving her in the first place.

"Come here baby." K-Killa ripped off his shirt like a male stripper and pulled his jeans of throwing them clear across the room. They landed on the floor.

"Don't any of these Atlanta bitches fuck me like you do. You know you got good body, baby." K-Killa said before he pushed his dick deep inside Dolorian's pussy, with force, making her moan and call his name like she was used to.

"I love the way you fuck too." She said, whispered, before she pulled her turquoise lingerie off, exposing all her goodies in their true form, ready to get down and dirty.

She saddled herself on top of his big hard dick and rode it like a wild stallion, as the sweat poured down both their bodies.

Just as she thought, she was about to cum. K-Killa beat her to the punch. He fell back on the bed as sweat covered his body. He begins to complain about being extremely hot and sleepy. Dolorian felt bad, knowing she had just poisoned his system with the gamma, she got from Peaches. All she could hear was Peaches telling her to use gamma with care.

"Baby I don't feel good." K-Killa jumped up off the big king sized bed running into the bathroom; he slammed the door behind him.

"Are you alright in there, baby?" All Dolorian could hear was K-Killa throwing up his guts like her girl had described at the Cheesecake Factory. She told Dolorian how in college her classmates gave a rape victim some gamma and it killed her after she threw up her guts. She shuck her head knowing she would defiantly have to go to church and repent for what she had just done. She knocked again, because K-Killa locked the door behind himself.

"Open the door Killa!" Dolorain yelled as she stood on the opposite side of the bathroom door, wondering if he was dead or alive, because silence had all of a sudden taken the place of the sounds of gagging

"K, open this damn door!" She screamed at the top of her lungs.

He didn't answer. Dolorain ran downstairs to the kitchen and pulled a butter knife out of the silverware drawer running back upstairs. She stuck it in the side of the bathroom door until she popped the lock. When she stepped inside the bathroom K-Killa was stretched out in the bathroom floor with white foam coming out of his mouth. His body trembled like he was having convulsions. She stood over top of him with the butter knife in her hand like a murderuos bitch. She knew she could get time and a lot of it for this one, if she let him die. Dolorian did what any woman in love, with a broken heart would do who had been cheated on would have done. She closed the bathroom door, got dressed and left the house. hoping that her revenge plot, she had just tested out on her own ex-boyfriend worked, and now it was time to take out the others like her and Dia, Sakina and Destini planned to do. She remembered a little sermon one of her mafia lap dance customers used to tell her. He told her, once a man killed; it's nothing to kill again. It became like a second skin.

"I bet the motherfucker won't hurt anybody else." Dolorain said, to herself as she sped through the streets of Atlanta, Georgia, at three o'clock in the morning. Scared to go back home, from the fear of being arrested for murder. She would have to ask her girls to help her get rid of the body because K-Killa was a sure enough goner. She feared he was dead.

When she went back to the house, Dolorian planned in having her girls by her side to help her get rid of the body. She drove through the street, something she was famous for doing lately, running over a garbage can as she pulled up into Sakina's driveway. She jumped out of the car in a panic; Even though the scheme turned out right she was still scared. The exterior she displayed like a steel grill melted away like yesterdays bad news. Dolorian ran up to Sakina's door knocking frantically, waking up sleeping dogs as neighbors. She held on to her black Gucci trench coat as she wrapped her arms around herself waiting for an answer. After standing at the door for ten minutes the living room lights came on.

"Who's that knocking at this door at 4 o'clock in the morning?" Sakina yelled through the front door.

"It's me Dolorian." She said like a crack head looking for some crack at 4 A.M. desperate.

Sakina's door flew open she stood there wiping cold out of the corner of her eyes as she watched Dolorian do a dope fiend move. She quickly locked all three locks on Sakina's door, the dead bolt first, then the knob lock. Then she latched the chain before breathing a word about what she had done. She ran over to the blinds in the living room to assure herself that she hadn't been followed, paranoia began to set in.

"Damn, Dolorian why are you out at this time of the morning? You scared the shit out of me knocking on the door like the police." Sakina said before walking over to the couch to sit down and wait for an explanation.

Dolorian walked back and forth before she could blurt out what she had done to K-Killa.

"What's going on Dolorian your scaring me by the way your acting?"

"I did it, Sakina." Dolorain said looking at Sakina with a crazed look in her eyes.

"What did you do, girl?" Sakina asked trying to investigate what her best friend had done.

Dolorain sat down besides Sakina to tell her, her deepest darkest secret. She had never committed murder before. This was like aphrodisiac that made her feel high, higher then life itself. So high she thought she would lose her mind.

"I killed K-Killa." Dolorian said as she squinted her eyes. All she could do now that the cat was out the bag was to confess.

"Stop lying Dolorain." Sakina said in a loud whisper. She knew this was some deep shit coming across her ears.

I'm not lying; he's lying on the bathroom floor back at my place dead. I told ya'll about the gamma at the Cheese cake Factory remember?"

"How come you didn't lure him into the hotel like we planned? How in the hell did he end up at your house dead on the bathroom floor? Did you fuck him, Dolorain?" Sakina asked.

· Dolorain had all kinds of feelings running through her body from chills; too hot flashes when her best friend asked her the one and only question that would expose her guilt. It was obvious she needed help for her human condition that suggests a girl bust a nut every now and then. She held her head down before gaining the strength to say that she'd fucked K-Killa brains out. If he wouldn't have died from the gamma, he damn well would have died from a heart attack.

"Don't tell me you fucked him Dolorian. You knew better to let him back in, that's like letting a vampire in." Sakina explained.

Dolorian sat there like an obedient child being chastised by her mother before she finally verbally admitted it.

"I fucked him, I couldn't help it. His wife called me after I left a message on her answering machine. She told me K-Killa had a sex addiction problem."

"What?" Sakina said as she moved a little closer to get all the gossip that spilled off Dolorain's lips.

"When I called him I asked him to come by the house like a stupid fool. I put on certain lingerie after he admitted he wanted me back and that we were going to celebrate getting back together again, I freaked."

"Damn Dolorian."

Dolorian spilled her guts to Sakina as she sat there being a pillow of support like a friend was supposed to. Dolorian told her how the sex was over powering; this made her want to do it even more. He made her fall in love all over again and she couldn't allow that.

"That's why you weren't supposed to fuck him," Sakina explained like she was an expert on the subject of pussy and dick. Dolorian grabbed hold of Sakina's hand.

"That's why I came to you Sakina, I knew you would understand this situation. I'm going to need your help getting out of this shit. I should have listened to Peaches, she told me to use the gamma sparingly and I fucked up. Temptation out weighted all other rules and reasons and the fact that the opportunity was there. If K-Killa would have turned me down when I invited him over, he wouldn't be dead now." Dolorian expressed.

"So what exactly is it you need my help with, Dolorain. You know I'm here for you like you was here for me when Wallace broke my heart."

Dolorian grabbed Sakina's hand extra tight before she laid what she needed on her.

"I need you to help me get rid of the body and all the evidence. If the police find out I gave him gamma, I could spend the rest of my life in prison, Sakina."

Sakina looked at Dolorain like she was crazy.

"Help you get rid of the body?" Sakina said before she let go of her best friends hand and stood up.

"That would make me an accessory to murder Dolorian. I don't know if I can do that."

Dolorian looked at Sakina with her mouth hanging open; she couldn't believe how quickly she had changed from the best friend in the world to a true bitch, showing her real color in a matter of minutes.

"Boy how we forget. I was there for you bitch when no one else was, when your man left you with a STD remember, and now that a bitch need a shoulder to lean on you switch up on me. I really don't appreciate that Sakina. I need you now and I expect you to help me."

Dolorain walked over to Sakina's mini bar and fixed herself a drink. While her friend waited out in her mind how much of her time she owed Dolorian.

"Ok, I'll do it. Let met me go and get my coat," Sakina said before she ran upstairs.

Dolorian and Sakina left Sakina's house to get rid of all traces of K-Killa being at Dolorian's house.

CHAPTER 7

Sakina stepped out of Dolorian's car walking slowly behind her. Dolorian struggled to put the key inside the lock of her house door; nervousness was a factor deep within her soul. She pushed the door open inviting Sakina in hoping she would make the discovery before she did.

"I'm not going in there first." Sakina said as she took one giant step backwards.

"Why?" Dolorain asked, scared but not showing it.

"I can't bare the sight of the dead, especially dead boyfriends."

"Why the hell are you tripping, after all Wallace is next on my hit list. So you might as well get use to it." Dolorain answered.

It was the wee hours of the morning just before dawn. The two ladies walked inside of Dolorian's dark house together holding hands, compromise was in order.

"Which bathroom did you say K-Killa was in?" Sakina asked as she looked around.

"Guess?" Dolorian said as she looked at Sakina for asking such a dumb question.

"I almost forgot, the one in your bedroom. I forgot you said you fucked him."

Dolorian cut the light switch on, as she looked down on the bathroom floor only to find nothing there but a puddle of vomit.

"Oh my god." Dolorian became estatic; there was no calming her down.

"Where is the body?" Sakina asked, as she looked around Dolorian's bedroom only to find nothing but crinkled sheets, where the fucking had taken place and Dolorian's lingerie on the floor.

"How in the hell did K-Killa manage to pull himself out of this shit. I gave him all the gamma Peaches gave me."

"I wish I could tell you where he went; only god knows. But where ever he is, I think you need to pack your shit and leave town, because there is no telling what he'll do to you once he catch up with you again. I thought you said you killed him." Sakina said.

"At least I thought I killed him. When we finished fucking he seemed to be totally bent from all the gamma I put in his drink. He collapsed and started foaming at the mouth." Dolorian pointed to the spot she left K-Killa.

"I can't tell." Sakina said.

"Look at all the vomit in the floor, that's proof enough I'm not lying."

"I never said you where lying, I just asked where is the body?"

Dolorian's nervousness seeped through her pores.

"I can't sit here like a sitting duck and wait for god knows who to snuff my black ass out. The plan is still alive, I'll just have to relocate til all this bullshit is over, and please Sakina what ever you do please don't mention this little episode to Dia or Destini."

"You have my word on that." Sakina swore.

Dolorian reached into her closet to produce a designer luggage set. She started pulling clothes out of the closet at rapid speed, throwing them into the bags, not caring that she wrinkled her five hundred dollar dresses and pants suits. She just knew K-Killa was out there somewhere and she vowed to find out where, or there would be no rest. Hotel 12 was the place she planned on lodging at until each one of the men she had a vendetta with was dead or disabled.

"I still can't believe K-Killa came back around, he was foaming at the mouth when I left here and now he's gone. There is no fucking way he left here alone, somebody had to help him. Dolorian said to Sakina as they tried their hardest to put two and two together.

"Now what Sakina asked, as she sat on the edge of Dolorian's bed watching her best friend go through the motions.

"I really don't know what to do now, shit is getting seriously scary, but since I promised ya'll we'd finish off our unruly ex's, I can't back down now. What would ya'll think of me if I backed down?" Dolorian asked Sakina.

"I don't think we'd think any less of you Dolorian, after all you're like a blood sista to me, Dia and Destini. We'd still love you no matter what happens" Sakina said trying to make her friend feel better.

Dolorian slowed down, turned around to give Sakina a hug. She felt as if no matter what happens now, she'd always have her girls there by her side to help her through the miry clay of all situations. Life had never dealt her a faulty blow like this one. This was some new shit, but like any strong woman Dolorian had her morals and principles and she planned on never abandoning her plans until they were finished. The first card had been dealt and now the playa would have to reveal their hands at this game called revenge.

Wallace sickness had him on an emotional roller coaster. The doctor put him on numerous medications, not to mention his weight was still going down hill. He battled everyday with his lover whom he left Sakina for. Wallace cupped his hands around his head as he wondered, had he infected Sakina with this deadly virus. He knew she hated him for picking a male lover over her. Wallace reminisced about the love him and Sakina once shared, until he decided to pack up leaving her in a state of turmoil.

"Damn, how did my life come to this?" He asked himself as he sat on the bed, him and his lover shared, since the break up of his four year marriage. Communication being the number one reason for the break up. All his hard work meant nothing now. His once upon a time handsome

face began to look frail. Just like his physique
when he looked into the mirror. He started to
look unrecognizable. The affection he craved from
Sakina was over looked and picked up by a male
lover. The baby him and Sakina lost weighed
heavy on Wallace mind He though back to how
he pampered her on the regular, with cards,
roses and candy, but nothing matter to her any
longer. He figured she no longer cared, so he
found someone who did and now this was the
result of his infidelity, aides> Full blown without
a cure. As he sat there he decided to make
amends with all the people he burnt bridges with
and the first person on the list would be Sakina.
The death sentence that made him weaker would
be the answer to all of the questions that
haunted his mind without rest. Wallace sat silent
as he watched his lover pack his belonging,
leaving him for another man.

"I can't believe your doing this to me after I
left my wife for you." He yelled in a soft voice as
he watched his lover take cologne bottles off the
dressers, along with his Brooke Brother suits
packing up to leave.

"You're the carrier not me. I'd be a fool not
to leave you now. Look at you, you're a hot mess.
You are just like anybody else now, gosh," his
lover said as he picked up his bags headed for
the front door.

"It's your fault I'm sick, if only when we
had the ménage a trios I should had used a
condom."

"It's just like you Wallace to fuck up, you
fucked over me, you fucked over your wife and

obviously your going to fuck over somebody else. I refuse to stay around and get fucked in the ass with your virus hovering penis."

Wallace and his lover's argument became heated, leaving Wallace all alone and in tears.

"I hate you bastard," Wallace said as he picked up a cologne bottle throwing it at the front door as it closed. When his lover left him to sulk and boil in his own juices. He picked up his cell phone not knowing what else to do.

Sakina picked up.

"Don't hang up." Wallace said in a sad whisper.

Sakina didn't, she remained silent as she watch Dolorian lock up preparing to leave.

"I'm sorry for the mess I made of our marriage. I just gave up trying to love you when you lost our child; your love had grown cold. I fought myself trying to resist the advances of other women and men all in the name of love towards you. I began to feel like less of a man, unable to satisfy the female agenda. I just want to say I'm sorry and I just want you to know that the disease I'm carrying is ruining my being. The person I left you for just left me all alone to pay for the crimes I committed towards you. Like they say Sakina, what goes around always comes back around again. I'm living proof of that." Wallace broke down; he started crying like a baby.

Before Sakina could answer Wallace hung up. A tear rolled down her cheek as she listened to the father of the baby she lost. It took Sakina a long time to come back from the depression and hurt, and now Wallace was feeling her pain. She wanted to tell Dolorian this like she shared everything else with her and the other ladies in her clique, but her heart wouldn't let her disclose this information. She feared being deemed crazy by Dolorian and the others if she would have told them that Wallace called. She feared backing out now no matter how crushed he sounded on the telephone. Sakina forgave him in her own special way. Deep down in the ruins of her heart love had nothing to do with what was already in action.

Wallace took a hand full of pain killers and laid down hoping to never wake up again. He prayed as he laid there asking for forgiveness for a whole list of sins he had committed through out his life. He hoped that someone in heaven or in another dimension heard his pleas.

"Is this what it all boils down too?" Wallace said before he gulped down a half of glass of vodka to chase the pills. His depression was deeper and darker than the depression that enveloped Sakina, when she feared having aides. She was redeemed while he was left all alone to face a death sentence.

Wallace kept saying over and over again.

"I can't believe it, I can't believe it, I can't believe it." While his brain walked through his childhood to his adulthood, then his manhood. Confusion set in creating a dark cloud that hovered over his head. He knew that a judgment must have been passed from up above for his life to have taken a turn for the worst.

Wallace drifted off to sleep, only to be awoke by a loud bang at the hotel room door.

"Management." A loud male voice yelled through the cracks.

Wallace tried to open his eyes only to find his eye lids heavy.

Boom! Boom! Boom!

He pulled himself of the bed, wrapping himself in a cologne filled sheet.

"Sir, your time is up here. Would you like to pay for a couple of more hours?"

"Wait a minute." Wallace picked up his Armani slacks off the chair, handing the manager of the hotel a fifty dollar bill for a couple of more hours.

"I'll bring your receipt back later sir." The manager said before he walked away.

"Fine Wallace said, still feeling the affects of the meds he had just taken. He laid his head down on the pillow and drifted off.

Sakina snuck into Dolorian's bathroom to dial Wallace number. This was the perfect time to find out exactly where Wallace was shacked up.

"Hello." Sakina said in the receiver.

"Sakina is that you?" Wallace said in a weak voice.

"Yeah, what's up with you? You sound funny." Sakina asked.

"Nothing, I just wanted to apologize that's all, Wallace said.

"Where are you? Wallace." Sakina asked.

"I been staying at Hotel Twelve, this sickness is really killing me Sakina. I don't know how much longer I'll be around." Wallace confessed.

"I'm sorry to hear all that, but you knew the risk when you left me for him. You never cared enough to look back." Sakina said in return.

Wallace hung up. The medicine took him under. Slipping into a deep sleep, but not that of death for destiny hadn't finished his job on him just yet.

CHAPTER 8

Sakina dialed Wallace number back, but no-one answered. As she waited patiently hoping he'd pick up. Dolorian yelled through the bathroom door.

"What are you doing in there? Sakina, Lets get the hell out of here."

Sakina stepped out the bathroom with a strange look on her face.

"What's wrong with you Sakina, you know I have to get out of here before the police and K-Killa show up at my door.

"I wasn't going to tell you this, but you did confide in me when you thought K-Killa was dead."

"What are you trying to tell me, stop beating around the bush and just tell me what it is you want to say?" Dolorian yelled! For she was already stressed out.

"Wallace called me just a few minutes ago." Sakina watched Dolorian's face, waiting for a response.

"I know you cursed that motherfucker out didn't you?" Dolorian asked.

"No, he sounded really weird; he told me that his lover left him and that the disease he's carrying is killing him. Then he said he didn't know what to do. I'm sort of scared for him Dolorian."

"What? You already know what aides can do and I know you know what aides can do to you. I know you didn't let that know good ass nigga lay a guilt trip on you, especially after he left you for a man!" Dolorian dropped her bags at this point.

"He's going through a lot Dolorian, I don't think I could add to what some unforeseen force is already doing to him."

"Listen Sakina, let me handle Wallace."

"Like you handled your man? That was messy Dolorian. If you would just put your pride aside and admit it. Suppose K-Killa brings the cops in about that gamma shit you did to him." Sakina couldn't wait to hear what Dolorian would say to what she had just laid on her.

"If that was supposed to be a disc, that was really low and if K-Killa was going to bring the cops they would have came for me. So get that thought out of your mind. So where exactly did Wallace say he was?" Dolorian asked.

"He said he's at the Hotel Twelve."

Dolorian eyes got big and round, for she would now be able to get Wallace, since she planned on getting a room at the same hotel. The two conversated as Dolorian drove like she was on a wild goose chase through the streets of Atlanta. Getting to the hotel was first and foremost on both the ladies mind. The traffic became thicker and thicker slowing down any kind of movement on expressway 75 & 85. The sun popped out the sky as Dolorian and Sakina sat side by side with distorted thoughts in each woman's head. Sakina gazed out the passenger window of neighboring cars as she looked over and spotted Destini & Boo two lanes over.

"Look at what we have here!" Sakina yelled as she sounded the alarm that popped Dolorian out of her mental rocky horror picture, playing off in her head. She was at the point of no return. She was contemplating as she sat silent with both hands on the steering wheel.

"What's up? Who do you see?" Dolorian asked

"Come here girl and get a good look for your self. And when you see them just remember that some of us are weaker than others."

Sakina knew deep down inside that the plan they plotted at the cheesecake factory in all reality was falling apart at the seams, even though Dolorian was dead set against her man. Dia's man, Destini's man. Her heart always out weighted the cons of it all. Boo could have crippled Destini, but she would still fall for his bullshit while laid up in a hospital bed. Wallace sickness out weighed the con's in Sakina's mind, even when she tried to play the renegade bitch, rolling with the best of them. Dia's stupidity, after being raped made her want Marcus back even though he called her a slut.

"Look at this bitch, she's back with Boo. Just last night she wanted that motherfucker blinded, now their fucking again." Dolorian said trying to read Destini and Boo's body language through the window of the car that sat next to hers.

"You can't talk Dolorian, just last night you wanted K-Killa's head and then you fucked him, so how could you judge her?" Sakina said.

Dolorian looked at Sakina as if she was crazy for bringing shit up while rubbing her face in it.

"Let's just follow them and and see what's up." Dlorian suggested.

"Just let them be, Dolorian," Sakina said.

Dolorian switched lanes as the cars in front of her blew their horns. She squeezed her automobile though the path of cars and trucks to get closer to Destini.

"You're determined to follow these motherfucker, huh." Sakina asked as her lunatic friend squeezed her bright red automobile where she wanted it.

All cars moved, once the traffic thinned out. The freeway became clear and all activity that ceased begun to move freely.

"Why are you so determined to follow them? Look at them their even laughing. Dolorian isn't that's a sign that somebody in that relationship is happy."

Dolorian didn't answer; she was determined to keep up, nothing Sakina said calculated in her mind. Sakina looked at the glare in her best friend eyes only to see the shadows of a woman gone stock raving mad.

"Dolorain, don't you think you have enough going on in your life right now?" Sakina asked.

Dolorian told Sakina to shut up as she continued to follow behind Destini's car. The car turned down Piedmont in Buckhead, a very famous part of Atlanta. Then it took a sharp left into the parking lot of one of Atlanta's most famous restaurants, Café Dupri. Cars where filling up the parking spaces, waiting like groupies to get inside.

"What the fuck!" Dolorian yelled as her temper exceeded its limit.

"Just forget about it. Dolorian, lets just do what we was about to do before I spotted Destinis and Boo. This shit your doing to yourself and them is totally unnecessary."

"Shut the fuck up, Sakina." Dolorian yelled as spit flew from her mouth on to Sakina's face. The rage she was in was unnoticeable to her, but very noticeable to the public eye. Sakina sat back in her seat and let Dolorian do what ever it was she wanted to. Shit was getting totally out of control and the course had already been set. There was definitely no turning back now.

"Damn, this bitch is packed. If we can't get inside now we'll just have too sit out here and wait for those motherfucker's to come out. Dolorian opened her purse and pulled out a pack of Newports, while her partner in crime watched on wondering when Dolorian would start smoking. She never even seen her with a cigarette and now she was smoking them.

The restaurant was packed. There was a select few who had made it into the V.I.P lounge. Dolorian watched from her car window as Boo wrapped his arms around the woman he had

Set up to be robbed and beat. Dolorian feared her revenge plot was turning into a love story with sex as always ending an episode.

"How in the hell could Destini defy us like this?" Dolorian asked as she sat there slumped in her seat.

"Maybe she's in love. Dolorian who are we to change all that?"

"Fuck love. Take a look at what love did to me; do I look happy to you?" Dolorian asked as she sniffled and sat back relaxed in her plush car seat.

She knew the wait would be long and drawn out, after all this was one of the most famous world re-owned restaurants in the city and she knew it was completely impossible to go in there creating a dramatic episode.

"Your right in your own eyes .Dolorian, who's to say that Boo and Destini didn't apologize to each other. I'm sure he didn't mean to hurt her like he did." Sakina's feeling she wore on her sleeve, not caring who could see it but only trying to make things right for a minute.

"What? You have got to be motherfucking stupid. Listen to you. What exactly did Wallace infected ass say to you on the phone; because what ever it was it sure got you all mushy now."

"I rather not go into details about what he said, but he did apologize, doesn't that mean something?" Sakina asked waiting for an answer.

"Hell no, he don't mean nothing to me. He's nothing; his loves nothing as a matter of fact. I just so happen to hate men now, all because of the shit K-Killa did to me. If I would have known years ago he had a sex addiction problem, I would have never fucked him. Look my whole life seems to be falling apart all around me. I danced and saved for years before I could save up for a brand new house, and buy myself a nice car and to buy all the nice clothes I always wanted. I never expected this married man to come into my life and change everything. My whole life has changed. Look at me Sakina, I can't seem to find my ass from my head anymore, shit has escalated into a bunch of fake promises, good sex and lies. The only thing missing is the video tape."

Dolorian and Sakina sat in the car waiting patiently for the breakfast crowd at Café Dupri to disperse. The restaurant manager showed up and when he did, people from out of nowhere ran asking when the owner would show up.

The crowd was so thick as if it was a concert going on. When Dolorian looked, Destini and Boo's car was gone. Dolorian took her hand and balled up her fist and started banging on the steering wheel madness had finally set in.

"Let's just do what we planned on doing when we stepped foot out here in the street. I'm sorry I spotted those two. I never expected you to act the way your acting." Sakina pleaded trying to get Dolorian to see things her way.

Dolorian finally broke down and agreed with what she was saying. She finally gave up her conquest and headed for Hotel Twelve in Atlanta Station, the destination she started on before she was rudely interrupted. She stepped out the car walking towards the Hotel Twelve doors. She walked up to the hotel desk ready to sign what ever forms necessary in order to get into one of the hotels room.

CHAPTER 9

Sakina's inquiring mind wouldn't let her rest; she had too know what room her unruly ex- Wallace was staying in. Dolorian grabbed the key card from the desk clerk bucking for her room. She had to make a couple of phone calls to the hospitals, from Southern Regional to Grady to find her unruly man. She couldn't believe all this shit was happening to her. She had to re-collect in order to handle what the world was about to dispense in her direction. She felt all alone even though Sakina was by her side.

"I'll be up in a minute Dolorian, I have to find out exactly what room Wallace is staying in," Sakina said as she made a quick move to the front desk.

"Go do your thing girl and when you finish I'll be in room 222."

"Ok."

Sakina stood at the front counter of Hotel 12 looking rougher than words could say. Her whole personality had changed since the Caribbean cruise her, Dia, Destini and Dolorian had went on. This man hunt was consuming a lot of her time from all the most important things that really mattered in her life, such as the rent payment, car payment.

"May I help you Ma'am?" the hotel manager asked.

"I need some information; I'm looking for the room Wallace Montgomery is in." Sakina asked.

"Wallace Montgomery, that name sounds familiar. Oh yeah, he's on the fifth floor. His room number is 523. Is there anything else I can help out with ma'am?" The manager asked.

"No thank you."

Sakina walked extra fast to the elevator hoping to get upstairs to see what Wallace condition was, after all he sounded pitiful on the phone. The elevator came to a complete stop as Sakina took a deep breath before stepping off. She walked up to room 523 and knocked. When she didn't get an answer, she became extremely worried rushing back down stairs to the front desk.

"Is everything alright ma'am? Did you find the room ok?" The manager asked.

"Yes I found it but there seems to be a problem, when I knocked my husband didn't answer. Is it at all possible you could let me into the room?" Sakina stood there looking like the same hot mess Wallace lover claimed he looked.

"I guess it will be alright since you say he's your husband."

The hotel manager walked to the elevator with Sakina and went upstairs. When the elevator stopped they walked up to Wallace hotel room door together.

"I hope he's here, maybe he was just sleep or something."

"Well you sure will find out in a minute." The Manager said.

He stuck the card in the slid before the door popped open. The manager walked away going back to his station at the front desk before another guest came in to register.

Sakina walked into the room where Wallace stayed. The room was dark and the air conditioner unit was blasting, even though it was quit nippy outside.

"Wallace." Sakina yelled out as she walked over to the bed, as she did she noticed Wallace bundle up under a blanket; his body appeared to be lifeless. Sakina cut the lamp on that sat by Wallace bed on a small wooden table.

Wallace." Sakina whispered in a soft voice.

She took her hand to shake Wallace hoping he'd wake up but he never did. She pushed him again hoping for a response but he still didn't move. Wallace's body felt cold and stiff. Sakina grabbed the covers pulling them back. She noticed Wallace body excretions all over the bed. The pills and liquor had done a job on him like Wallace prayed for it took, Sakina to make the gruesome discovery. Sakina covered her eyes as the tears begun to flow down her face. Wallace's death changes a whole course of events about to take place. She picked up the phone to dial 911 for the police and coroner to pick up the body. She did the only thing she knew to do; she covered the body up with the blanket Wallace slept under trying to be the pillow of strength like a wife was suppose to be.

"Wallace, why did you do it baby you could have talked to me about what ever it was you was going through. All you had to do is say it to me when you called earlier tonight." Sakina talked to her dead husband's body like he was still alive. This brought flashbacks of her own suicide attempt. She knew once Dolorian got wind of what was happening, she would be happy about the whole situation.

This was Dolorian's mission to play her hand at being a god, taking out all the men who had done her wrong when they crossed her path. Dolorian expected K-Killa wife to answer the phone once she dialed his number, trying to be incognito but his wife didn't answer, he did.

"Hello?" K-Killa said when he picked up the phone.

Dolorian could tell his spirit was weak and broken when he picked up the phone, from the way he sounded on the other end of the receiver. She held on in silence until she decided to hang up. A prank caller, an ass hole for not responding when he said hello. Dolorian became extremely scared when she heard K-Killa voice on the other end of the receiver. She wondered how in the hell did he end up back at his wife house in Florida in a short period of time. She vowed to herself she'd get to the bottom of this one way or the other, if it was the last thing she did on this blasted planet. Shit was already too wicked in her life at this point and time. She already felt as if she was living her life on the edge like half the population in Atlanta, Georgia. She always knew she wanted to live in Atlanta, ever since she was a young girl. She always dreamt of dancing on stage but would have never dreamt it would be on a stage at strip club in the ATL.

K-Killa blew her mind the first time they fucked. She never expected them to make love and fall in love. Pride, envy, jealousy, hate and all the other feelings associated ran through the blood in her veins. Dolorian threw her cell phone across the room, mad at the world for what was happening in her life. Dolorian also dialed Destini's number to let her know she seen her and Boo on the expressway headed for Café Dupri's.

"Hello?" Destini answered.

"Yeah, Destini I see you and Boo is back together now. What's up with that honey?"

"What?" Destini answered.

"You heard me, I thought me and you Sakina & Dia had an understanding, we even made a pact to that effect or do you have amnesia now?" Dolorian said.

"Dolorian, I know we made a pact ever since the Caribbean cruise. But you me, Dia and Sakina always did things together and we always said we would do a lot of things together, but this I never thought you would do. I went home that night after we met at the Cheesecake factory and I really thought about some of the things we talked about. Some of the things we in our drunken rages I thought long and hard about it and I'm defiantly out Dolorian. I looked around myself and I've come to terms with all the stuff me and Boo been through together and I'm not willing to let him go no matter what he did to me. Everytime I look at the scare he left me with, his face pops into my mind. All and all Dolorian, I need my man, and yes of course me, you, Sakina and Dia been friends for a long time now. But I'm here to tell you girl, I don't think I could ever find another man like Boo.

"Destini, are you listening to the words coming out of your own mouth. You sound crazy girl. Are you still planning on going under the knife or have you changed your mind about that too? Boo must really got you whipped over there, for you to be back fucking him.

Backwards. I can't believe you decided to go back to Boo for another robbery and ass whipping."

"Listen up Dolorian I have to go and one other thing since you disapprove of my choice in men. Loose my fucking number bitch!" Destini clicked her phone off once she ended her long time friend ship with her ex-friend Dolorian.

Dolorian bit down hard on her teeth as she hung up the hotel phone and picked up her cell phone off the floor, before placing just one more call. The receiver of the call Dolorian had placed answered, but the music was so loud in the background you could tell there was a full blown party going on.

"This is you know who and I know you know what to do." Peaches yelled into the receiver when she picked up the phone.

"Peaches this is Dolorian."

"Hi, honey how's everything going?"

"Not so good Peaches. I did everything you told me to, but it didn't work. Where exactly did you get that gamma?"

"What! Where arc you?

"I'm at Atlanta Station at Hotel Twelve. If you could come over I would really appreciate it," Dolorian said.

"I'll tell you what. I'll be right there. What's your room number?" Peaches asked.

"222 Peaches and please come, this is really an emergency."

"Capise honey, I'll be there."

Dolorian sat on the bed staring into space. She opened up her bag pulling out a valium before lighting another cigarette. She decided to take two valiums to calm her already jittery nerves. The pills mellowed her out. She wondered when Sakina planned on coming back. Dolorian knew she went to check on Wallace but all the while Dolorian hoped Wallace didn't talk Sakina into coming back to him, like Boo did. Destini knew Sakina tried to play hardball even though she was straight up, suburbia material. The streets of Atlanta was too much for Sakina but Dolorian knew how fast Sakina could flip the script and become mushy and romantic, letting love drive her crazy in love. Dolorian knew Wallace's sickness was eating him alive. She feared Sakina giving in and ending up with the short end of the stick again. Like always she seemed to end up with, no matter how nice Sakina appeared to be. As Dolorian sat there feeling like she was trapped inside Hotel Twelve, a soft knock was at the door. Dolorian feared going outside since she heard Killa voice on the phone.

"Whose there?" Dolorian asked in a soft voice.

"Peaches honey."

Dolorian popped off the bed like a jack in the box. She couldn't get to the door fast enough.

When she opened the door Peaches was standing there in a purple Escada dress. Dolorian took one look at this tall transvestite and took one step back. Peaches were hot. She out weight any woman, to Peaches there was no competition. Because when ever she stepped into a room thugs, husbands, boyfriends, uncles, fathers and sons always was on her dick. She rocked a higher quality of clothing then Dolorian. Dolorian became immediately jealous when she opened her hotel room door and the bitch that sold her the counterfeit gamma stood there at her door like she didn't have a care in the world. Peaches shape even looked like that of a woman. Her sex change operation gave her the permission she needed to fuck who ever she wanted too, when ever she wanted too and where ever she wanted too. Peaches were use to women clutching their boyfriend's arms when ever she came around. Dolorian stepped to the side as Peaches swung her hips from side to side, walking pass her. Before Dolorian could say a word, peaches begun to talk.

"What's the emergency honey; I gave you enough gamma to do the job unless you're trying to kill a horse. So exactly how many gamma pills did you give your problem?" Peaches asked.

"Those pills you gave me were bogus! I'm running for my life because of you." Dolorian opcncd up her valium bottle and popped another pill in her mouth.

"Bogus, honey nothing I do is bogus. I give the best. Bogus, never. As a matter of fact why would you say that?" Peaches asked as she slipped her purple gloves off her hands.

"I gave the problem I was having a substantial amount of the pills he appeared to be going through fits, so I left. When I returned to the house he was gone instead of dead."

"Dead, you never told me you were trying to kill nobody. You lied to me and now you have the nerve to be complaining. I'm not willing to go down for a murder one rap for you."

"Why exactly would you give me counterfeit gamma."

Peaches was talking but the words coming out of her mouth Dolorian didn't want to hear. Dolorian walked back and forth as she listened to Peaches act as if she wasn't the distributor of the shit that had her scared K-Killa was going to kill her.

"All I can do honey is give you some more. Is that what you want?" Peaches asked.

Dolorian became silent. She had visions of trying it again but this time, the gamma would work. At least it would in the slide show in her imagination. Then she thought about her life and how she wasn't ready to die, especially by the hands of a man. But before she could think straight she blurted out.

You could make this up to me Peaches, since I'm on the motherfucking run, is get me a 45"

"What are you talking about honey?" Peaches asked.

"You know Peaches, a gun."

"A gun." Peaches jumped out of her seat.

"You have got to be kidding, ain't no dick worth going down like a sinking ship. You got it bad honey and all I can say is good luck, because Peaches is getting the fuck out of here. " Peaches looked at Dolorian like a crazy psycho bitch before she opened the door and stood under the frame of it.

"Your letting dick bring you down and all I can say to you girlfriend is, if the dick is that good that it has you loosing your mind. That's a sign that it time to let the dick go."

Peaches closed the door behind her self, as she walked quickly to the nearest elevator. She wasn't willing to let the lifestyle she built up from the floor up go, to do a life sentence for Dolorian. Peaches could tell Dolorian was playing herself out. Her ego was blown up and it went straight to her head. To Peaches this was the starting gate to the road of destruction and to this zone Peaches was not the gate keeper. Dolorian stood there frozen in her tracks. It was like she was paralyzed in her steps. She thought about the questions she asked Peaches concerning getting a gun. If her life was to be safe and remain that way she figure K-Killa would have to go. He was the reason she was about to live her life on the run like a fugitive, all because he loved to sling dick and his wife allowed him to do so. A gun was a piece of cake to get down on Simpson Street where robberies occurred in the broad daylight. She would have to pull herself out of her shell and find a thug to get the instrument she swore would protect her from any and everything she faced.

CHAPTER 10

Sakina hailed down a cab headed back to Hotel Twelve where she left Dolorian in turmoil. Sakina knew in order for things to go straight forward now she would have to do some real soul searching. Wallace wasn't the problem now, the problem would be Dolorian. She knew Dolorian was going through some shit that seemed like there was no returning from. Sakina didn't want to get caught up in her mess, so she would either have to cut her off or help her. As she set in the cab headed back to the other side of town, she thought about how she would be able to help her. Sakina wanted to go all the way with Dolorian, but she knew how wild Dolorian could get Since working at the strip joint. Another thought that ran through her head was the fact that once Dolorian sat her mind on something or somebody she would go to extremes to get what she wanted, no matter what it was.

Dolorian sat on the side of the bed once again wondering what her next move should be. She needed a gun and was going to get one if it was the last thing she did. She planned on taking to the streets to find the right thug to put this cold piece of hard steal into her hands. Dolorian thought about the men she bragged so much about that night at the Cheesecake factory. The gangsta's she told her best friends about. These boys being the baddest of gangsta's on the streets of the ATL. John Gotti didn't have nothing on these nigga's. They would shot to kill their own mother's if they had too, to get what it was they were trying to obtain. Cocaine, Heroin, Meth, and a variety of other drugs. These gangsta dealt and Dolorian would be the one to know. Especially since she used to sniff after doing lap dances for the leader of this notorious crew. She watched as they flocked into the club she danced at. Twenty Deep and as they did all the dancers in the club. She would invent dances to get those nigga's attention. She sat there on the bed reminiscing about the first time she did a lap dance for one of these crew members. She remembered the many lap dances she did in a room that was dimly lit. The leader of the crew he always insisted that Dolorian stick her pussy in his face when ever she did a dance for him. It was like he was addicted to the smell. Dolorian broke into a cold sweat just thinking about it. She knew she would have to stepped foot out of her room sooner or later. So she showered and changed her clothing into something stimulating and sexy. So she put on one of her most sexy number as if she planned on dancing again. Dolorian picked up her phone calling this thug she knew could help her get exactly what it was she wanted, that being a gun.

"What?" The sexy thug said when he answered the phone.

Dolorian stayed silent for one minute then she answered, since it was her who was placing the call.

"Sham is that you baby?" She asked as she sat on the side of the bed with a smile on her face and a body filled with valium.

"This is he, what can I help you with?" Sham asked.

"I need to come see you Sham. This is Dolorian. I know we haven't seen each other in a long time but I feel a meeting is in order."

"What did you say your name is?" Sham asked as he breathed hard into the phone receiver while Dolorian made her peace.

"Dolorian you know, the one who use to do private lap dances for you down at the club."

"Dolorian, it's been a long time baby. What can I do for you?" Sham asked.

"Can I come see you? I really will be needing your assistance, Sham."

"Well Dolorian, I think that can be arranged. When is the soonest you can come down?" Sham asked as he continued to breathe hard into the receiver of the phone, like he had asthma. His huffing and puffing into the receiver made Dolorian wonder had this nigga been smoking the crack he'd been selling.

"I'll be there in one hour."

"I'll be waiting."

Dolorian grabbed her purse and headed to the lobby of the hotel. As she ran out of the lobby, Sakina who had just returned from the hospital, paying her last respects to Wallace ran up stairs, as Dolorian ran outside.

Sham confirmed Dolorian's theory, anything she wanted she could get including a gun. Sham vaguely remembered Dolorian. He had had so many lap dances, blow jobs, and ménage a trios. Dolorian was just dust in the wind to him. Pussy came a dime a dozen where Sham ruled. ATL being his stomping ground. If anything went down from the North side of boulevard to the Southside College Park. Sham and his squad would be the one's who executed the orders from Indian Creek to Bank head. There wasn't a square inch of Atlanta, including five points that Sham didn't have his tentacles in. He was like the king of Atlanta.

Sham sat back in his theater chair in his mansion in South Atlanta, calculating in his mind. Was Dolorian snitching now for the Feds or what? He couldn't be too careful, because he hadn't heard from her in years. The phone calls from out of the blue shuck him up a little. His lieutenants stood side by side at the entrance way to the theater room in Sham's house. His phone continually rang as if he was the President of the United States of America. His status in the streets was very important, being down with some of Atlanta, Georgia's most dangerous gangsta's in the industry. This made him graduate to another level extremely quick.

"Rosco, do you know a Dolorain?" Sham asked his paid employee. Rosco stood over top of Sham like a watch dog very attuned to his surroundings. He only answered questions when asked, never volunteering information.

"Dolorian. I don't recall the name," Rosco answered with his hands behind his back in a parade rest position. Sham remained seated as his phone continued to ring with him answering only on occasion.

Dolorian felt a rush of power as she took off her clothes. She changed into a black leather outfit, by one of her favorite designers Gucci. With the thin skinned leather coat to match. She had an appointment with one of the most important nigga's in Atlanta and she knew, first impressions were very important. Dolorian thought back to how Sham use to use his big hands to grab her around her hips, when she rode his dick through his red monkey jeans. He would just sit there and let her take complete control, doing the one thing she did well ride. Dolorian laughed to herself like a Bella Mafia Bitch that had connections in a town where networking was king in the ATL.

Her pussy became moist just thinking about it. She felt as if she was slipping back into darkness just hours ago and with a push of a button all that was about to change. If the meeting between her and Sham went well, all this was about to change. Her pussy would pay the tab for the favor she was about to ask Sham. That being to assassinate K-Killa, while he laid in the arms of his ignorant wife. Dolorian put the finishing touches to her make up and slipped on a pair of five hundred dollar black haired pony boots, to set her expensive outfit off. She grabbed her black Gucci clutch purse throwing one of her outfit she use to dance in into it, hoping to set the mood when Sham laid his sexy almond eyes on her beautiful brown frame. Dolorian knew since she hadn't stripped since K-Killa swooped her off her feet, there was a possibility she would be again before the night was over.

Sakina stayed at Dolorian hotel room waiting for her to come back from where ever it was she stepped off too. She grabbed the remote control starting to flip through channels, trying to find something suitable to watch. Sakina mind couldn't rest after witnessing the first hand attempt of suicide. It was like god was trying to tell her something by putting Wallace back in her life while he went through the exact same thing as she. Her heart became extra heavy as she released tears, thinking about life and how it use to be then. She thought about how she wished life could be.

CHAPTER 11

Sakina stayed in Dolorian's hotel room waiting for her to come back from where ever it was that she ran off to. Grabbing the remote to the television, she started flipping through channels trying to find something suitable to watch. Sakina's mind couldn't rest after witnessing a first hand attempt of suicide, it was like god was trying to tell her something by putting Wallace back into her life while he went through the exact same thing she went through. Her heart became extra heavy as she released tears thinking about life and how it had nothing much for her. Sakina thought about how it use to be and then how she wished it could be. But all in all, she still came up empty without a resolution to any of her problems. It was like her unruly ex was trying to call her from the grave.

"I can't sit around here and wait for Dolorian, I have a life to live." Sakina clicked off the hotel television set before grabbing hold of her purse heading home.

Dolorian started her candy apple red BMW headed to South Atlanta. She had no fear in her heart being around gangstas for the duration of her life. She knew how to seduce the best of them. There wasn't no man that hard that he couldn't be soften up. When she arrived at her final destination, she pulled up to a big black gate that protected Sham and his squad from the police, feds, DEA and CIA agents. If some just so happened to come calling, plus neighboring gangstas that wanted a piece of the pie that Sham created from out of nothing. Building an empire wasn't an easy task, at least not where Sham was raised in Bankhead Atlanta, with a mother heavily addicted to the most dangerous narcotic, like heroin and coke. Sham had to grow up and become a man at a very early age, 7 to be exact. There wasn't nothing,Sham's boy's wouldn't do for him. When ever he laid a command it was followed to the very letter 8, 9, 10, 11 and 12. All his boyhood years were spent scouting out neighborhoods. He could set up trap houses. This is how Sham got his start in the business.

He considered and interviewed his soldiers that wanted to roll with him like they was applying for a job at Publics or Pizza hut. If they didn't fit his criteria they wouldn't be let them in, what turned out to be one Atlanta, Georgia's most dangerous squads. Controlling city blocks from zone to zone. Sham's squad eventually took over, rubbing elbows with other black young males who had made it out of the hood. From hustlers to rapper's and gangster's, these people being already well connected in the town where the desperate come to be discovered like in Hollywood.

Dolorian pulled into the gated community, searching for an address she was given by Sham. She found it. She stepped out of the car straightening her clothes, after all she knew the kind of females Sham rolled with always top of the line ho's. He was living proof that no matter where a brother or sista success came from. He was never that far away that you couldn't just reach out and grab it. Dolorian pressed the door bell as she stood there patiently waiting to be answered. When the door finally open, instead of a maid in a cute black and white outfit, or a butler. A tall black thug holding a glock answered. Instead of a friendly hello he searched Dolorian,with his eyes, without saying a word before stepping to the side. As Dolorian's body was being scanned, and her body temperature and reaction weighted out. The test to enter Sham's home, was approved. The glock was instantly put away while Sham's lieutenant disappeared out of sight for a minute, while Dolorian stood there in the middle of the floor with her arms folded waiting for Sham to appear, like the magician that he was.

"Dolorian." He called out when he stepped out of the shadows.

Dolorian quickly turned around looking him directly in the eyes in a seductive manner. After all, first impressions was very important on this night. Because she needed Shams assistance and expertise on how to lay a no good ass nigga down, that being K-Killa and Marcus. Only if Dia didn't give in to him like Destini. While her and Dolorian was absent one from the other.

"Sham, it's been a long time." Dolorian greeted him licking her already moist lips.

Sham stepped out of the shadows once he seen Dolorian's face. He remembered her.

"Now I remember you Dolorian. You was one of my favorite dancers Sham said, as he told Dolorian to follow him. He walked down a hall to an adjoining room where the walls were painted emerald green. Dolorian looked around to see the décor of the ready made millionaire's house. This made her ready to get the negotiations on the rode. She hoped that in her mind the body fucking she planned on doing to Sham would get her what she wanted. She knew she passed the first battery of test and that there would be many more to come. All this just so she could get what she came there for in the first place.

"So, Dolorian I don't have to tell you I was shocked to hear from you after all, I haven't heard from you in a couple of years and out of the blue you call. What's a thug to think?" Sham sat down waiting to hear the answer Dolorian was about to sip his way.

"All I can say is out of all the thugs I fucked, you was the best and I figured it was time for a repeat visit. And I also have a favor to ask you."

Sham sat there silent for a minute. He knew there was something else behind this visit, him being the man he was he seen it all. He had made too many deals and put out too many contracts on peoples lives, not to be able to read Dolorian's body language.

"Well, Dolorian you're no different from none of the other's that shows up out of the blue to ask for favors. But before I can even listen to what it is you have to say, you'll have to assure me your not wired."

"Wired." Dolorian asked.

"Yes, wired." Sham said as he sat in his chair leaned to the side, waiting for Dolorian to change her mind.

"Well, I guess I don't have a choice but to give you the proof that you need." Dolorian took her leather jacket off and handed it to Sham. He called his lieutenant in to search the jacket for wires and mics, just incase Dolorian was working for some unknown source. But the search wouldn't end there.

Sham turned his eye contact back in Dolorian's direction, giving her the go ahead to strip down to another piece of clothing. That being her Gucci blouse. Dolorian started to unbutton it slowly. She gave her watching audience the feeling that she was concealing something. When she took it off she handed it to Rosco, Sham's lieutenant. Saving Sham the trouble of doing it him self. He twisted in his seat, for he never saw it coming.

"I'm sorry to be the one to inform you but you'll have to take those off too. With you being a stripper in all, that shouldn't be hard to do."

Dolorian looked at Sham and then his lieutenant.

"Not with him in the room, he'll have to go."

"He works for me. He'll be staying just in case, after all Dolorian it's been years."

Dolorian was caught between a rock and a hard place. She couldn't leave now for she was in too deep. Plus Sham wouldn't allow it. He had a battery of test already mapped out in his mind and if Dolorian expected to ask for a favor and get it, she would be permitted to past each and every one of the test.

Sham's body guard stood over her with his brown muscular arms crossed, like a statue ready to kill on demand if told to. Dolorian kept her eyes on both men as she lifted her leg to step out of her thong. Then she reached behind her back to unsnap her bra. Each piece of lingerie fell to the floor leaving her standing there wearing nothing but her shea butter slick skin that no wires or mics were taped to. She held both arms up in the air before she bent down spreading her ass cheeks, revealing her tight ass hole.

"Alright, that's enough." Sham said as he grabbed hold of his dick through his designer jeans. Dolorian knew exactly what to do to turn this hard core thug into a willing participant.

"Get her clothes." He told Rosco. Rosco gathered them up handing them back to Dolorian. She dressed as quickly as possible.

She stood there in the middle of the floor re-dressing. Being on your P's and Q's was a tough job, but nobody mastered it like Sham.

"Can I tell you the reason I came here now? that you know I came here in peace." Dolorian asked, as she buttoned her bra back and slipped her thong's back on her heart shaped ass.

Sham cleared his throat. He was ready to know why Dolorian chose his squad over any other, to do her dirty work.

"Why is it that you're here?" Sham asked, as he sat at attention.

"I need a gun and I don't have no where else to turn."

"A gun, huh, I thought you said you came in peace, now you want a gun." Sham laughed, Dolorian made him break out of his tough interior for a minute.

"If you don't mind me asking, why it is that you want a gun."

Dolorian didn't want to disclose that information so quickly.

"I'm having a serious problem with my man."

"So you want a gun, because you're having man problems?"

"Yes."

I don't think that's a good idea to put a gun in the hands of a hostile woman." Sham said as he laughed once again.

"I'm not hostile, just a little desperate that's all."

Dolorian explained as she plopped her ass in the chair across from Sham.

"How come I'm getting the feeling your not telling me everything?" The room became extremely silent. Dolorian held her head down for a minute, for she knew for her life was put in a position, where things were being entangled in a world of uncertainties.

"I'm going to tell you like this Sham. My man used me up like a dirty dish rag, Then he left me.

Then I found out that my man wasn't just my man, but another woman's man, also that being his wife."

"So what you're telling me is that your man was married even while you were fucking him."

"That's exactly what I'm trying to say. He really hurt me and I want pay back."

"Well Dolorian, me and my squad don't usually take on domestic disputes. That's just something we don't do here. My operation is geared towards a whole nother direction and I feel if I help you with this, I'll be wasting precious time. This thing I'm running here is strictly dope, money, respect and power. A type of operation as you can see. I thought you knew this."

"You thought I knew what?" Dolorian asked.

"I thought you knew from the word on the street what we do here. Helping desperate woman tame their boyfriend just ain;t one of them." Sham and Rosco laughed at Dolorian for bringing this to them.

"Maybe there's something I can do to change your mind." Dolorian cocked her head to the side looking quit cute to Sham.

"What is it your willing to do to make me see things your way?" Sham asked, trying to see just how far she was willing to go. He snapped his fingers instructing his lieutenant to be dismissed from the room.

Dolorian was at her wits end. She never imagined her vendetta scheme would bring her this far. Never did she see herself sucking dick to get help with a problem. She waited until the secret room to Shams office was closed before she fell to the floor on her knees in front of him.

"So, you want to blow me off. Do you think this will make me take the job?" Sham asked all the questions. This was a part of the test that he mapped out wanting living proof that Dolorian wasn;t working for the DEA or the FBI. After all, bitches sucking dick to get in wasn;t changing Sham's mind. He could get his dick sucked anywhere by any woman he choose. Dolorian wasn't creating no new moves, that all women couldn't do, if push came to shove. Sham, like any man, let her express herself. If licking him made her feel convincing then so be it. He threw his head back as Dolorian unzipped his jeans releasing what looked like 101/2 inches. She shoved it into her mouth as she watched Shams eyes roll back in his head. Sham moaned, he loved pussy, especially from dancers, because they knew how to move their bodies, selling their style to the highest bidder. in this case this blow job would open doors and end lives in Dolorian's mind. But the only thing she didn't know is that Sham was a lower rank in a long string of commands. She would have to go through him, to get to the main man of the whole TBM, That being Meachy. She never knew she was sucking the wrong dick.

Stroker's, Magic City & The Blue Flame turned out some bad bitches. If Sham told the story of the stripper chronicles that landed in his lap on many occasions.

"Suck it." Sham said as Dolorian's eyes rolled back in her head at the same time Sham's did.

Dolorian finally deep throat it, hoping for an academy award when she finished. She had to get Sham addicted to her if K-Killa was to be put to rest once and for all.

CHAPTER 12

Destini & Boo relationship became quit strong after the break up. Destini still contemplated going under the knife. Everyday she scuffled and saved to clear up the mistakes Boo created in the first place. She was sorry she had to end the relationship with Dolorian and her other girlfriends, but she had to do what she had to do in order to block out all the, I told you so's that was to come.

Boo continued doing the same kind of work he did before even considering a relationship. Robbing drug dealers was his forte and number one trade. And he vowed he would never give it up, until caught by the police or popped by the hands of one of his drug dealer victims. Destini did as she normally did when it came to her mans activities. She turned the other cheek. She had no idea what dealers had been robbed by Boo or that the dealers was looking for him. She had no idea that the word on the street was to bring Boo's head to Meachy, dead or alive. She put herself at great risk by bringing him back into her home. Just as long as Boo laid his pipe like a true dick slinger, anything he did or said was alright.

"I still love you baby, ain;t nothing changed" Boo said, before grabbing Destini. Hyping up her dress. He fucked her from behind while she cooked his dinner. fried chicken and macaroni and cheese. Like a fool, Destini turned a deaf ear to the truth and fell goo-goo eyed for that man that set her up to be robbed, leaving her with a destroyed eye to prove it.

"I want to be with you again like I use to be. Just promise me something." Destini said, in between moan. Boo was tearing her pussy up from the back, when he answered her pleases in moans and groans.

"Are you listening to me, Boo?" Destini asked as her body was pressed up against the wall, next to the stove while Boo continued to thrust.

Ah....Ah... Boo moaned, not paying attention to one words Destini managed to slip off her tongue. When Boo released himself, he stuck his penis back in his pants grabbing a piece of chicken off the stack that Destini had just made for him. She stood there dick whipped, unable to speak. Boo had left his impression on her. When Boo released himself, his moans were still enlarged in her mind. She wondered deep in her mind, has she made a tragic mistake, when she told Dolorian to loose her number. After all, Dolorian might had been right about Boo, but Destini's scared face kept her mind zoned in on the way she looked. She was blind to the fact that her man she was still in love with was a true dog. Boo walked out of the front door without saying a word. Destini's heart walked out the door right behind him. She stood there wondering where could Boo had left to go. Then she figured he went out to his car to get something. When she looked out of the window Boo was nowhere in sight, neither was his vehicle in its parking area. Destini showered and laid there thinking in her big king size bed, all alone on the edge. Not knowing if her man really loved her or was he just using her house and her, to do his dirt out in the streets. Bringing back god knows what from the hood. She became scared as she laid there not knowing if he was out robbing drug dealers, putting her life in danger once again like he did once before. Destini cried to herself as she laid there knowing how hard it was to find a man, let alone a good one. Her body or pussy wasn't getting any younger, not to mention Atlanta was filled with models, ho's, prostitutes, transsexual, and god knows what else. A man could find pleasure just about anywhere. This made women her age take extra pride in the men they attracted to them, and who had been with them for years. Destini's good paying job and her worldly possessions meant nothing to her without someone to share them with. She feared Boo being intimidated by the success she made for herself, when he walked out on her leaving her to die at the hands of some of his street thug buddies, the first time around.

Boo pulled into one of the most dangerous streets on the Boulevard. This was the block that never sleep, like little New York. Soldiers patrolled this region of the city on the regular, using gorilla tactics to get a point across. The police even changed shifts three times a day. But on the Boulevard sleep didn't exist. This was the place dope was sold, pussy was bought and contracts were set up. Guns were sold, recruiters recruited, while transsexuals tricked. He stepped out of his car full of confidence, while walking into a trap house to scope out the floor plans. The plan was to set up the green dope dealers new to the area. They wouldn't have known what was coming. Their status on the block was so green they didn't even know who Boo was when he stepped in the door. He entered the dirty resident without a stocking cap over his face. Boo pulled a rubber band filled with twenties and tens out of his pocket throwing it on the table.

"Hey, man I don't know you like that to be selling you no weight." The new dealer said.

"No problem man, I don't want no trouble." Boo said, as he grabbed hold of his money and the rubber band that concealed it. Little did the dealers know Boo had gather all the information he would be needing in just a matter of minutes, and now they would be added to Boo's target list later on that night.

Boo walked extra fast to his car headed back to Destini's house to wait this one out. She would be fucked in each and every position to keep the blinders pulled over her eyes to what it was that her man was doing in the street. Boo walked up to the door knowing it was pass ten o'clock and that his woman was in bed. He snuck up to her bed room and laid down beside her with his clothes on. Destini tossed and turned until she opened her eyes.

Boo, get out of my bed with those dirty clothes on. She said as she pulled the covers up to her chin.

"Come here baby give me some more of what I like." Boo knew how to tame his woman, all he had to do is tell her he loved her every once in a while and she would do and be what ever he wanted her to be.

Boo did as Destini ordered. He stripped down to his boxer shorts and laid down beside Destini in the pitch black darkness, holding her in his arm with robbery on his mind. As he laid there he waited patiently while watching the clock until Destini rolled over falling back to sleep. She had to get up early the next morning for work. Boo moved very careful, afraid that he would wake Destini. He grabbed his jeans holding on to the chains attached to the belt buckle. He slipped them on his body, but not before grabbing hold of a black stocking that belonged to Destini. He stuck them in his pocket. Before he took to the streets, he looked over at his woman sleeping peacefully not knowing if he'd ever see her again. After all, living life on the edge was a bitch, but somebody had to do it. Boo left the house hoping that the new drug dealers made enough cash for him to steal. So he and his woman could lay back and take a cruise if the spirit hit them. If shit went well, Destini would be able to quit her job and lay back just the same.

Little did Boo know that the drug dealers he was about to hit up was down with some of the baddest gangasta's in the ATL, that being The Black Mafia. Boo got in his car started it up ready for take off. He reached under the seat pulling out his weapon of choice, that being a Smith&Western. hoping once inside the trap house, he'd be able to take who ever was inside down all by himself. When he pulled up to the BLVD, the trap house was filled with fiends buying dope that was said to come straight from New York City, where the crack was said to be more potent then that in Atlanta. Boo waited until he spotted one of the dealers leaving the house. This was the opportunity Boo thought he was waiting for. He walked up to the front door knocking softly like a bitch.

"Wait." The voice from inside the house yelled out. Boo stood there with his S&W underneath his coat ready to shoot once he entered the house. The door flew open and Boo was invited in. He eased his way inside the house not knowing if things changed since he scoped shit out earlier.

"What up, man," the door man yelled out, once he let Boo inside closing the door behind him.

"Cool, man, cool." Boo responded as he stood there with his hands inside his coat pockets.

"What you need man?" The door man asked. He remembered Boo from his visit earlier to the trap house looking for some weight.

Boo looked around before he staked his claim.

"Can I use the bathroom, man?" Boo asked before he made the attempt to pull his piece out.

"Yeah man hurry up."

Boo walked down the long dirty hallway, lined up with trash bags and empty bottles.

"Damn." Boo said, as the smell of pure urine hit him in the nose before he could even open the bathroom door. Once the bathroom door closed, Boo pulled his S&W out of his pocket double checking for the bullets in the chamber. Everything panned out. Boo burst out the bathroom with Destini's black stocking over his head waving his gun in the air.

"Get the fuck down." Boo yelled.

"What the fuck." The door man yelled, hoping that his boy in the back room would come out with his piece in his hand, shooting any and everything that moved.

"Where is it?" Boo yelled in the door mans ear.

"What man?"

"Where's the fucking dope and the fucking money?"

"I don't know man, I just open and close the door for these fiends. I don't know anything about any dope or money."

Boo didn't want to hear no more. He knew if he wanted shit done he would have to do it himself. So he took his big silver gun hitting the doorman over the head. He fell to the floor. Boo locked the front door and headed down the hall to the closest in the bedroom. When he pushed the door open. One of the dealers laid there snoring with a sawed off shot gun in his arms. Boo peeped this. He counted the drug dealers snores before he entered the room. He spotted the money all piled up and wrapped in plastic. Boo knew he hit the jackpot. He and Destini would be able to lay back for at least a year or two. Boo had all kind of erotic thoughts running through his head. He grabbed a pile of the wrapped cash headed for the front, but before doing so. He pulled his stocking cap off, which was the wrong move. Boo ran down the hall bucking for the front door. As soon as he grabbed for the door knob he heard the click of the shot gun and a loud boom. The bullet hit the wall given him a chance for escape.

Hey nigga I know you." The gun man said as he clicked his gun again ready to make another attempt to shoot.

Boo ran for his life, jumped in his car taking off through the streets. Once he noticed that no one was chasing him he stopped pulling over to the side of the road, on the expressway taking a deep breathe and saying a pray. The shot gun blast scared the shit out of him. Boo knew he had nine lives like a cat, eight of which had already been spared. The only thing he regretted pulling off was the stocking cap before he fled the scene. The voice in his head kept blurting out.

"Hey nigga I know you." This scared Boo. He wondered how could these new dealers know him, after all he never seen them before. Boo dismissed the thought, got out of the car putting the freshly wrapped money out of the trunk before going home to Destini like nothing ever happened.

CHAPTER 13

Dolorian's laid the best sex Sham ever had on him. He knew deep down in his heart that he tricked Dolorian, making her think that he was somebody he wasn't. All the while knowing that Meachy was the leader of this notorious squad and that he was nothing but a mere watch dog just like Rosco. Power wasn't running that rapid in the streets for the power trip to continue in Sham's mind. Meachy gave him an inch and he took a mile, walking around with an inflated ego that got him paid.

"So, how did you enjoy that?" Dolorian asked, as she wiped her mouth with a handkerchief Sham handed her.

"Don't tell me you're finished. You didn't do anything." Sham said as he stepped out of his pants.

"I just blew you off, how could you say I didn't do anything."

"I know you can do better than that. There is no way your going to tell me you're expecting me to give you a gun for that." Sham said watching Dolorian's face.

Dolorian knew if she was to walk out of there with what she came for, she better had laid something better than a blow job on him. So she took her clothes off once again. When she finished she saddled herself on top of Sham.

"Is this what you want?" She asked, as she began to move slowly up and down, riding his dick with her eyes closed. Acting as if this was an illusion.

"Come on baby, You've been dancing to long now. So you got to know how to fuck."

"Excuse me" Dolorian said, as she tried another move she knew all men loved. She stood up and bent over, giving Sham the permission needed to enter her from the back.

"That's exactly what I'm talking about baby. I knew you had it in you, it just needed to be released, huh?"

Dolorian didn't say a word, she just enjoyed the moment. Just as the love making was getting intense, Meachy burst through the doors. He, and what looked like a string of trained killer soldiers. The United States Military didn't have nothing on these nigga. They all walked in without saying a word. Meachy was a big strong man. Dolorian's heart fluttered as she looked at him and how tall he stood.

"What's going on here?" Meachy asked as Sham quickly straightened up his clothes.

"I was just helping this young lady that's all." Sham said while pulling up his Red Monkey Jeans.

"We don't conduct business this way. So young lady you'll have to go," Meachy said.

Dolorian felt extra stupid after sucking a strange dick.

"If this isn't his house whose house is it?" Dolorian asked

"This is my house. Don't tell me you didn't know that when you came here." Meachy said as him and his soldiers stood at ease like military soldiers.

"He told me this was his house and that I could get help with a problem I'm having. That's why you walked in on us in a compromising position." Dolorian explained.

"What kind of help were you looking for?" Meachy asked Dolorian.

"I came here because I'm having trouble with my man, and when I told Sham my story he promised he would help me."

"What? What could he help you with. We don't get involved with women's problems. The only problem we could help you with, if you were having this problem is community problems. Are you having problems in your community?" Meachy asked.

"No." Dolorian answered.

"Well then we can't help you. I would suggest you gather up your shit and leave my house." Meachy said, as his biggest and strongest soldier stepped forth just incase Meachy needed help putting Dolorian out.

"But I just blew him off, and now you're telling me I can't get any help. Oh hell no." Dolorian went off. It took two of Meachy's bodyguard to move her towards the front door.

Meachy looked at her and laughed. He knew this was a wild one and he didn't want to attract no trouble. So he decided to listen to what it was Dolorian wanted to say.

"I'll tell you what, step in my office so we can discuss this in a business manner." Meachy said, like the business man he was.

Dolorian walked two steps behind Meachy as he stepped into his office. His office was decorated like a Military Captains office with war like statues and pictures on the wall, including a picture of Scar face, The black panthers, and a variety of other hero's.

"Have a seat." Meachy said.

"I'm sorry you had to find us in this position. But I'm kind of desperate right now."

"And why is that?' Meachy asked. For he wasn't trying to tell Dolorian anything, but just listened to her needs and wants, like he was so use to doing to each and everybody who had ever asked him for a favor. Dolorian's nervousness shined through. Meachy could see her nervousness. She was shaking when she made her confession, but all of this was more than necessary.

"Dolorian, how exactly is it you was led to me and my operation?" Meachy asked. He knew Sham had already put her through the test to know whether or not she was worthy of his time.

"I remember your lieutenant from the club, he use to come by quit regular to get his lap dance on."

"Oh really, so you're a dancer."

Meachy sat back in his swivel chair as he put both his hand together.

"Is there a possibility I could get as lap dance?" Meachy asked, trying to see how far Dolorian was willing to go.

He smiled knowing he was the man and he never had a problem getting what he wanted from a woman before. Dolorian wondered when she would finally get what it was she wanted. She had already sucked one strange dick tonight. Now Meachy the TBM squad leader was practically begging for a lap dance. The whole shit was turning into a joke. Nobody handed Dolorian what it was she came there for yet, which was a gun.

"Well Meachy, do I have a choice. If it takes a lap dance to get what it is I came here for then so be it."

Meachy clapped his hands dimming the lights in his office. He couldn't wait to see what Dolorian was working with. She stood up revealing the terrible Gucci wears she sported. She took off her black lamb skin leather coat and laid it on the chair. Then she stepped out of her Gucci skirt and thong. She knew if she wanted K-Killa head on a silver platter, pussy would be the appetizer. Then maybe just maybe Meachy would like what she was about to do well enough to help her with her problem. Meachy touched a button behind his desk and music blurted out of a speaker in his office. Dolorian knew it was now or never, if she wanted to make an impression. This would be the time to do it. Meachy laid back doing a shoulder lean in his swivel chair, waiting for the games to begin.

"If you want me to dance for you, you're going to have to put that chair in the middle of the floor." Dolorian said, as she stood in the middle of the floor butter ball naked. Meachy gave her the power she needed like a dominatrix. To give the orders and set the commands and she liked it. Meachy possessed a power that many men find quit hard to obtain. He had the power of influence, bringing about change in many peoples lives that he managed to touch with or without their permission. Along with this, he also possessed the power of persuasion. He could put out a word or a roamer, and in a matter of minutes it would spread through out the hoods that he controlled, finding its way in some of the most critical parts of the community. The power of force, using violence was another one of his mighty tactics. He ruled over young men's lives ranging from age seven to fifty, moving them with military might. He knew the secret to it all, that's being all subliminal. He even imposed himself on the weak, making him self strong even when the weak tried to resist.

His neighboring enemies only wished they had what Meachy had. How the matrix in their minds wouldn't allow them to find their way out of the labyrinth of life in the hood. Everyone wanted to be a hustler, but nobody seemed to be as lucky as Meachy. He sat on his throne watching, waiting and wanting Dolorian, as she moved her body to the music. She twists and turned her hips from side to side, feeling him in-between her legs even before he could touch her. He wondered on, as he contemplated. Could Dolorian turn him on, after all, there was a certain kind of woman that Meachy liked and only god knows they were lined up at his door on the regular. Wishing and hoping to be down by law with him and his squad. In this game he didn't know who to trust. Your brother could be your little brother one day and your worst enemy the next. Meachy had no fear of death. He knew he was born to die. But planned before he left this planet to be Americas most wanted gangsta with his closest homies by his side, fresh out of prison and the hood, to enjoy the fruits of life.

As Dolorian danced right in front of his face, he stretched out in his seat. He was tempted to reach out and grab her but knew this wasn't permitted. But after all this wasn't a strip joint but his home, where he paid the rent and if he wanted, he could just take Dolorian's phat pussy if he damn well pleased. And that's exactly what he did. He pulled Dolorian on top of him before she could finish dancing and undid his pants.

"What are you doing, this isn't a part of the deal."

"What deal? We don't have a deal just yet." Meachy disclosed.

Dolorian looked deep into Meachy's eyes when she landed in his arms as he pulled her on top of him.

"Your man must have hurt you mighty bad to make you sort me and my squad out to help you."

"He did. I never imaged it would end the way it has."

Meachy took his lips and planted them on Dolorian's. She gave into his lead. She wouldn't dare fight it, this was the one to her. He would be able to bring this whole vendetta and revenge plot to a stinking head, once and for all.

"I didn't think you wanted to fuck me. I thought you just wanted to hear me out." Dolorian said, as she found herself sitting on another big black dick butterball naked and this one felt right.

"Why would you want to hurt ole boy. Why didn't you just leave him?" Meachy asked

"I don't know. I just thought he loved me that's all, but I guess I was wrong."

Dolorian knew if she expected to get full help from this one. She would have to come clean and confess like she did to Sham. It wasn't like Meachy never heard a story like hers before, after all he was like the black Michael Colioni of Atlanta. He had power all over the streets and if he thought Dolorian;s pussy was good, she was willing to use it like an American Express card all over his ATM dick. Meachy made Dolorian know what a real man felt like in between a woman's legs. When he finished doing it to her, she could have sworn she was in love.

"What do you want me to do to him, for what he did to you?" Meachy asked as he pulled his penis out of her. Dolorian thought about it for a minute. She put her arms around him and explained what she had tried to do to K-Killa and what she wanted Meachy to do to him, since what she tried had failed.

"I gave him some gamma and I thought he had died. I left him laying there to try to find somebody to help me move the body, but by the time me and the help returned to get rid of all the evidence the body was gone. Meachy sat there content, listening to what Dolorian was saying. She sounded truly twisted to him.

"So what you're telling me is, you already tried to kill home boy. You're the bold one, huh." He said laughing

"He tried to destroy my heart, then I found out the bitch had a wife along with a sex addiction problem. To top it all off, he has a child by this bitch."

"Damn." Meachy said. "I'll tell you what, since you laid that good ass twat on me, I have no choice but to help you out."

Dolorian was happy now. Her point had finally been seen by a real man with power and intelligence.

"Where exactly does this nigga live?"

"In a Spanish Villa on the beach in Miami."

"I'll send a couple of my boys over there and show that nigga that he can't come to Alanta doing none of our woman any ole kind of way. Shit doesn't work like that. See now we can call your problem a community problem. Because there is no telling who else he did that shit to. Like you said, the nigga's got a sex addiction problem."

Dolorian stood up. Leaned over and hugged Meachy, for her wishes had finally been granted.

A James Hickman Book

CHAPTER 14

Dia called Marcus on numerous occasions. She knew he had to have a soft spot in his heart for her, no matter how hard he appeared to act, by hanging up each and every time she called. She was determined to find that spot. Dia hadn't heard from her girls since the Cheesecake factory and doubted if the plans they all planned together was still in affect. She hadn't a clue that Dolorian was going insane over her man, or even that Dolorian had tried to kill K-Killa. Dia was left in the dark to fin for herself against the demons that rose up inside of her. Telling her to call Marcus, with out support, a junkie will relapse and that's exactly what she did.

Marcus being the thug that he was it was hard to break through his tough interior. He always displayed the" I don't want to be bothered attitude". Dia's girls was the only ones who could make her see the light, that night at the Cheesecake factory over drinks. But once the drinking, plans, laughing and crying was over. The dark clouds of reality always seemed to roll back in. Dia parked her car at Marta, to take the train for the first time in her life. She didn't feel like dodging in and out of traffic on this Friday night. She stood there looking at the train tracks, wondering if anybody would give a fuck if she threw herself in front of the northbound train when it finally arrived. Then she popped out of it when she opened her cell phone to try to call Marcus number for the hundredth time. Wishing he'd have a forgiving heart like hers. When she dialed the number, the phone rang before her call was immediately dropped. The train finally pulled up as she stepped inside the last car and took a seat. She gazed out the window as the train rode quickly down the tracks making her dizzy. Dia stepped off the train when the train reached her stop. Men whistled and hollered at her as she walked through the turn style. But none of these men appeared to be as strong as Marcus. The rape episode in Rod's basement had left her shook up for a long time. But what ever it was Marcus wanted, she had no problem giving it to him, like any other woman would have. Even though he turned on her like a vicious pit bull. Dia never stopped or tried to give up trying to get her man back, even though he treated her like a dog. She was just one of those women who had a forgiving heart and she never seemed to understand why men seemed to not have the same kind of hearts.

Teaching school and being around lots of children was the only thing that could make her smile these days, especially after being humiliated and sexually abused by big grown men. She tried dialing Marcus number once again hoping and praying that the prayer she prayed to get her man back would finally be granted this night, for she was tired of being lonely.

"Hello?" She said in a soft whisper.

"Whose this?" Marcus asked. For getting how his ex sound on the phone.

"It's me Marcus I was hoping you would answer. How have you been?"

"I'm putting up with it."

"Have you forgiven me yet?" Dia asked.

"Yes."

"Good, I was calling to see if we could get together for drinks at Club Compound?"

"I guess I could join you."

"Great, Marcus I never meant to disrespect you in any way or embarrass you that night."

"Listen, let's just forget about that."

"Only if you tell me I've been forgiven."

"What time do you want me to be at the club?"

"I'm in that area of town now, how about you swing by now, if you're not too busy."

"Alright, I'll see you in twenty minutes."

Dia's smile was so wide she looked like a patriot of the Mona Lisa. She knew he would come around and finally he did. Clud Compand was packed. When Dia arrived it was ladies night out and all drinks were half off. She took her seat at the bar as she watched her Timex watch. She counted down until she saw her Ex-walk through the door. But he didn't. Twenty minutes passed still no Marcus.

"Can I get you a drink?" The bartender asked.

"I'll have an orgasm." Dia said.

"You, and half the women in here." The bartender said before fetching her drink.

The bartender filled Dia's glass with all the proper ingrediance to cause an orgasm. Then to top it off, he added whipped cream. Dia sipped on it. Getting whip cream all around her mouth.

"No baby that's not how you drink that." A woman said sitting two barstools down from Dia's.

"This is how you do it." She had no problem demonstrating.

She took the shot glass, opened her mouth wide and without using her hands she circled her lips around the glass until she had a grip. Then without warning, she threw her head back swallowing everything from the liquor to the whipped cream. Letting the contents slid down her throat.

Now that's an orgasm." She said before slamming the shot glass on the bar.

"Let me try that. I never had one of these before until tonight. I always heard people talking about them." Dia said.

"Be careful baby girl, an orgasm ain;t nothing to play with. These drinks can get you truly ripped." The strange woman announced.

Dia drank four orgasms before Marcus finally decided to walk through the barroom door. His twenty minutes turned into to forty minutes. By the time he got there Dia was drunk and ready to fuck and had an full blown orgasm.

Marcus walked into the bar with a ho on his arm. Dia stopped dead in her tracks when she spotted him. She thought her eyes and her mind was playing tricks on her, because the ho was white.

"Marcus. over here." She yelled across all the music and laughter going on.

Marcus pimped his way across the floor still with his arm around this woman, and Dia wondered why he would bring another female with him. After all she wanted to make amends with him and get her man back.

"Whose she?" Dia asked, as a spark of jealousy rose up inside of her.

"Oh her, she's my friend I wanted you two to meet. Me and her we have an understanding."

"What do you mean Marcus, I wanted to see you alone. That's one of the reason's I asked you to come down here to meet with me."

"Well I'm not alone, as a matter of fact I'm in to a new type of lifestyle since we broke up."

Dia looked at Marcus, wondering what in the hell he was talking about. But just couldn't piece together what it was he was trying to say to her.

"I'm into group sex now. You know. Ménage a trios."

"What? I can't believe you would even come down here and tell me no shit like that. I thought you wanted me back like I wanted you back and this is the way you respect me."

"Let's not even go there. When it comes to respect, I'm surprise you would even use the word. After all, you fucked all my homeboys while you was on your period. So don't stand there and talk to me about respect Ho." Marcus said.

Dia felt like a piece of crap by the time her ex man got finished with her.

Marcus style had changed along with his lifestyle. He wore the fliest of clothing now and he also upgraded his taste in cars. Dia knew at this very moment she would be totally secondary in his life. Her shyness and laidback attitude wouldn't exceed what Marcus was now into. White ho's. She figured he was still living in the pass at the time when the white man tried to talk to her, and he became extremely jealous.

"I was hoping you would have loosened up, since I last saw you. But it's obvious you haven't" Marcus said, while his white ho stood there by his side giggling shaking her head at Dia, for being such a pooput.

Dia felt really stupid as she stood there wishing she was sober enough to take the train back to the station where she parked her car,only if she could remember which station it was.

"If I knew you were playing the role of a pimp I would have never called you." She said, getting loud attracting attention.

"I'll tell you what Dia, why don't you find us a table so we can talk about it. It's obvious you beat us to the punch, I can see your some what tipsy."

Dia pointed across the room to a table that was not occupied as her and Marcus and his white ho walked toward it to take their seats.

"Ménage a trios huh. What made you start fucking white bitches, wasn't black pussy enough for you? Dia talked, as if the white girl wasn't even there ,looking Marcus dead in the eyes.

"I just love pussy. Lets just say that, and one other thing. Don't knock my lifestyle until you've tried it."

Dia became silent as she felt the full effects of the orgasm she drunk, before Marcus arrived. She was saying things that she wouldn't normally say'

"I have a room right down the block. After I order a couple of drinks, I want you to come on and go with us. Where did you park?" Marcus asked, trying to convince Dia to go with him and his date.

"I'm not driving I took the train." Dia answered

"That makes shit that much better." Marcus said, as he reached into his pocket and pulled out a bundle of hundred dollar bills. Dia wondered, was he selling dope now since he never pulled out that much money while he was fucking her. Why did it take a white girl to bring all that out of him. He laid the money on the table before he grabbed hold of Dia's hand and looked into her eyes making her want him even more.

"Come on and go with me." Marcus said in a soft seductive voice.

Dia wanted him back no matter what, and if this was the way to get him back, she was willing to try to do what ever he wanted.

"You see baby I live my life by codes now. With all the diseases out there a fellow can't be too careful and one other thing, I want to share all this with you baby. So come on and give it a try. You'll never know, you might like it. Dia thought about it for a minute. This was something new and she was tired of being all alone. She couldn't see herself going home to grade papers on this Friday night. She needed a little spice in her life and if Marcus though she'd like it, she was willing to give it a try. If she could get him back. She looked over at the bar where the strange woman who showed her how to devour a orgasm sat. The lady held her drink up in the air to salute Dia, for finding herself someone to give her a real orgasm. But little did this stranger know Marcus was a real true freak, who was so caught up in his own sexual gratification he wasn't capable of giving her an orgasm.

"So what is it going to be?" Marcus asked as his white ho sat there still grinning, waiting for Dia to make up her mind.

"Ok." Dia said, while she held her head down. She knew if word got out about this it could ruin her whole career as a teacher.

Marcus orders a bottle of Alize and Patron to take back to the hotel with him and his two freaks. He was going to show Dia the time of her life, for the first time in her life.

"Don't worry, I'll make sure you get home safely after I screw your brains out." Marcus said, as he laughed. It was like every word that came out of his mouth had an effect on Dia .She felt the effects like she had taken an ecstasy pill. She just craved his touch like never before. She knew there was competition now in the form of white flesh. Something that all men seemed to crave, after a successful bout in lives. They all walked down the street as the wind chill made Marcus grab his white girl, leaving Dia to fin for herself. Something she was getting quit use to.

CHAPTER 15

Dolorian knew the goals she planned on meeting, had been met as of this moment. Even though Meachy asked her to leave because something else came up, didn't mean that he would push her problems to the back burner. She felt positive. Things would turn out on a positive note even if blood shed would have to take place for K-Killa to understand just how serious Dolorian was. She laid in her hotel room in deep thought playing out a whole list of dramatic situations,.Love stories, independent modes and moments, In her thirty something years. Out of all the men she ever fucked, for some strange reason she just couldn't stop thinking about Meachy. He fucked her like a true soldier with honors. He made her feel special when he held her in his big muscular arms, screwing her like it had his brand and label on it. No sex ever made her feel this special; Meachy made love to her and listen to her problems all in the same hour. The power he held over all the other people turn Dolorian on. He knew how to hypnotize his subjects. The more relaxed Dolorian begun to feel about him and his decisions, the more confident she began to feel and comfortable when ever the chance would arise, for her to be in his presents. If he wanted too, he could bend her into doing his will. Whether the urge being sexual or on a gangsta bitch level. No matter what part of town Dolorian came from, she could always blend in. She knew a man of Meachy's status could make a woman do what ever it was he wanted, including licking the crack of his ass if that was his desire. Power could make any bitch drunk and he had it.

What it all really boiled down to was the people in the zones. Meachy controlled all, wished they could be like him. He understood their values, their spirit and their taste, thus making it easier for them to fall under the spell he was trying to cast. The very spell that gave him the power he needed to step up and take control of the streets. Dolorian closed her eyes drifting off to sleep knowing that the following day would hold much surprises. After all Meachy promised her he would make what K-Killa did into a community problem and their was no doubt in her mind that Meachy was feeling her. Just like she wanted to be felt.

Word got back to Meachy that there was money and dope stolen from one of his many trap houses. But the money and dope wasn't taken by any ole stick up kid. Word spread pointing all fingers in Boo's direction. It took only five minute for the buzz to spread in the streets concerning the contract on Boo's life. Just as Soldiers were given jobs titles as look out men, each and every large family that had more than ten children was put on alert promising the rewards for locating and executing a thief in the community. Boo broke the hustler code that penetrated the air in all the zones North, South, East and West. Always, watch your brothers back without stabbing him in it. Boo robbed too many of Meachy's soldiers and not to mention a couple of Meachy's rival's in the hood, without the guilt it took for him not to show his face in the streets. The following day by setting up the next dealer. Destini's life would be put in the cross fire this time. Meachy's soldier's all loaded up their cars from Benz's to Cutlass Supremes. Each and everyone of them was armed with weapons, guns, sticks, knifes what ever it took, they had it, not to mention a couple of Cherry balms. They went out like military soldiers ready to wage war on the bold bad niggas like Boo, who would steal from his own mother if the spoils looked good enough. Battles meant nothing to a man like Meachy, he battled all of his life after being brought up in total poverty. It took a lot of family feuds, and out and out killings to stay on top. If this is what success meant and selling a soul to get what he wanted, then this was how it was going to remain. He knew his soul was long gone but that wouldn't stop the fight he found his self in each and everyday. Taking those who was willing to go down with him to the levels they all lived their lives by, hell bound.

The ride wouldn't take long to reach Destini's house where Boo was shacked up sleeping peacefully. The money had been safely put away, but the money that had been stolen from Meachy wasn't taken by Boo. But by some one else, That being an opportunist who saw an opportunity and took it. Boo turned over crutching his arms around Destini not aware that Meachy's soldiers were headed on that side of town, with strict orders to bring him to Meachy, dead or alive. The cars slowly crept down Destini's suburban block. The squads had a hard time finding the address considering each house on the block resembled each other, like that of the stetford wives. The only difference was, Destini's house was the only one that held a dysfunctional nigga like Boo under lock and key. The dirt he did on the regular in the street put Destini's house into a class by it's self, marked as the red alert danger zone.

Meachy's main lieutenant Sham stepped out of his cutlass that was sitting in front of Destini's house on twenty fours. His outfit told the story dressed in grey, black and white from head to toe, with his ear piece sticking out of his ear waiting for what ever new orders to come across the air waves. As he pimped to Destini's front door he maneuvered twelve lower ranked soldiers, that all marched in formation directly behind him with their hand gripped around semi automatic weapons, waging a war with the enemy. These men and women were trained to carry out executions, also known as hits without even as much as batting an eyelash. They wouldn't give a hoot how Destini or Boo felt, while the punishments were about to be hand out for the crimes Boo committed to his own brothers in the community where Meachy managed. Boo fell to realized that he took food out of the mouths of drug dealer's babies and children each and every time he committed a crime against the chosen few who rained on the streets.

Boo sleep walked through the dark hallway headed to the bathroom. He reached down to pull the toilet seat up, that's when he noticed a shadow running pass the bathroom window. But before he could break away from the toilet to retrieve his S&W a hand came from the darkness grabbing hold of his mouth dragging Boo's body out of the bathroom before he could even know what hit him. Boo's body was dragged down the hallway. As the rug burned on his heels they caught on fire. He was pulled up to the front door before he could bread. His body was transported outside and shoved in the back of the cutlass Supremes truck and the hood slammed down on his head. Destini was not so lucky. Before she could wake up to realize what was happening all around her. She could see this definitely was a kid napping. Before the cars could crank their engines, the trunk was opened and Boo dragged out of it. He stood before the one who gave the orders to put him in it, Sham.

Where the hell is Meachy's money?" The heavy voiced and big hand soldier asked. But Boo still wouldn't answer.

"I don't know what you're talking about, man." Boo responded as he stood there looking surprised as the squad stood there in his face. But the question was, whose squad was it. Boo had no idea Meachy sent his squad to confiscate what rightfully belonged to him. Boo had definitely crossed the line this time.

Man, what the fuck is going on here? I don't have any money or drugs." Boo said, responding to the sawed off shot gun pointed at his left cheek bone.

Destini's body was held down with the mighty force of a big black elbow. She knew what ever was going on had to have something to do with her no good ass boyfriend Boo. She knew at this very moment she should have taken Dolorian's advice, after all Dolorian must had seen this coming for her to feel she had to forewarn her best friend. But the matters of the heart ruled out over years of friendship. She decided to let the throbbing feeling between her legs control her thinking. Boo had caused enough trouble in Destini's life. But this right here was defiantly it. Destini struggled to free herself from the clutches of the unknown man whose elbow was still embezzled in her back, but her attempt was of none effected.

"What exactly is it you're planning on doing to us, man?" Boo asked.

"I was ordered to kill your mother fucking ass man. But since I'm not in the mood, I'm taking your black ass to Meachy."

"Meachy?"

"Yeah, Meachy."

"I don't have no beef with Meachy, so why exactly is it your taking me to him?"

Boo asked waiting for an answer. This sudden abduction scared the shit out of him, just like the shot gun blast after he robbed the Blvd dealers on this very night.

"Meachy said he want your black ass dead or alive. Now what I'm about to do to you is take you back inside the house, so you can get Meachy's shit and don't for get the money." Sham said, as his soldiers all looked in Boo's direction. Ready to shot his ass if that's what the next order spit out of Shams mouth appeared to be.

"I don't have no dope or no money man. Some body's trying hard to pen this shit on me man."

"I'm going to say this one last time, Where's the shit and the money?"

Boo didn't say a word it was like his whole body shut down. He swore he would faint. Boo didn't say a word he vowed he wouldn't and so he didn't. He had plans with the fresh green stacks of cash. Destini was held down in the same position with her cheeks pressed against the cold leather seat. She wasn't use to the flipside of the street life. This was Boo's life and not hers. She decided to beg these men for her life, for she had nothing to do with this and she wanted out.

"I don't know what's going on here, I had nothing to do with what ever it was he did." Destini explained to the hard core soldier standing over top of her. He looked at her and said.

"Bitch, shut the fuck up."

Meachy meant more to this soldier than life it self and here went a cold blooded bitch without a heart, stealing from the one man that fed him, when his mother was too high, and when his father decided to leave home taken a whore on as his lover, instead of his drug addicted wife, this young soldier seen some shit. Destini mind would never be able to comprehend this. She went as if the world revolved around her in her big ass house. He hawked and spit on the ground as he pulled her out of the car headed back for the house. The money would have to be turned over or an execution was being created right there in front of Boo and Destini's face.

"Hay wait young brother, I'll give the money back, I promise. Only if you promise to let me and my woman go."

Sham looked at Boo and laughed.

"Oh, no son. That won't be happening on my shift. You stole from the wrong mother fucker this time son and I'm going to show you exactly what I'm talking about.

Destini was carried over to the corner of the living room as Boo stood there with his boxer on without a tee shirt, looking like a skinny teen age kid, about to get his ass kicked after school. Destin didn't breath a word of defense on her mans behave. She was totally fed up with Boo and his secret operations behind her back, putting the whole house in harms way. She decided to sit there and watch him get his ass whipped.

"How about her, Sham?" The soldier asked as he stepped over top of Destini, holding a glock in the palm of his hand.

"She can watch her man get his ass kicked." Sham stood there in front of Boo as his hand signaled one of his bosses highly trained and paid twins do a double twist and karate kicked right in the center of Boo's chest. He fell to the floor. Destin turned the other cheek as she seen all the pain and suffering the squad put Boo through for the thievery he committed to their boss Meachy.

"Let me do her." The young soldier said as he stood there looking at Destini in her big brown eyes with hatred. But not hatred for her, but the hatred he felt for his own mother that each and every woman he ever been with associated with, dated or seen. She put them through hell reenacting in his mind on the constant basis, the struggle he been through all of his life like hell.

Boo looked up at Sham, pointing towards Destini's bedroom. Everybody knew at this very moment she was down.

"I knew this bitch was down with this shit, she probably drove the getaway car." The young soldier said as he cocked his gun ready to put a big hole in the side of Destini's head.

Destini started screaming, she went off.

"I knew you would do this shit again, look at what you've done to me. I'm tired of this shit Boo, your crazy." Destini said.

"No bitch we already know you was down with this chump nigga. So don't try screaming your way out of this shit now." The young soldier said waiting for Sham to give him the go ahead to pull the trigger.

Sham pushed the young soldier back before he picked Boo up off the floor and pulled him back to the front door and put him back in the truck headed for Meachy's house.

"How about her, aren't you taking her?" The young soldier asked.

"Hell no, Meachy said. Bring this chump mother fucker. He didn't say bring her so let her go."

Destini knew God had to have been smiling on her shoulders like never before. He spared her life once again from the man she had let in to her life to tare it apart, like he attempted to do not to long ago. Destini cried and fell to the floor when she heard the cars pull off from her driveway. As she looked up and put both her arms up in the air spreading them to the sky, praising her maker up above. Hhe loved her more than any man and his actions spoke louder than any words Boo could have ever said to her. She decided at this very moment that she would dedicated her life and earthly possession to God, because after all he is the one who saved her life once again from a situation no earthly man could.

CHAPTER 16

Dia and Marcus stood on the elevator gazing at each other like they were both strangers in the night. She thought back to the night of the rape. But then let the thought go in her mind, for she knew if she ever brought that up again Marcus would never forgive her. Hotel Twelve was the hotel Marcus took Dia to, hoping that the Ménage a Trios they was about to have would leave him satisfied. Marcus had sort of an obsession, when he really though about it. He loved sex and he knew this was turning him completely out, since he told Dia to kiss his ass leaving her labeled as another rape statistic. No woman had ever embarrassed him like she had especially in the front of all his home boy's and he wanted revenge just as bad as she did. He thought about it and planned on getting it this night. Dia let go of all the dirt Marcus had ever put her through in order to be a man's lady, she would have to conduct a serious composure.

"Are you ready for what I'm about to do to you?" Marcus asked, with sex on the brain. It was like his life, a turn in the worst way.

Turning sex into an everyday sport, just so he could get his rocks off.

Dia giggled. She figured Marcus would come to his senses and loose the white chick he perpetrated, especially once they all got into bed to conduct the Ménage a trios that she figured was just a secret fantasy that he had to act out like most men. Dia knew her man couldn't have forgotten all the crazy love sessions they had in the past, there was just no way. Marcus opened his already paid for hotel room door, as if he had been planning this for a long while. Dia stepped inside only to find a spread all around the place. Marcus white ho's clothes were all on the back of chairs on the bed and when she looked into the bathroom, she spotted her accessories all over the place and her panties hanging over the back of the shower pole.

"Can I ask you this Marcus before I attempt to do this?" Dia asked. She tried to whisper but Kim was right there.

"What is it baby? Don't tell me your going to back down now." Marcus said, as his white girl sat down on the side of the bed as if the conversation was geared in her direction.

Dia didn't know what to do, so she just blurted it out, what she was feeling as if she was wearing her heart on her sleeve.

"Are you and this white girl in a relationship?" Dia asked, as she parked her body against a wall like a wall flower waiting for an answer. Marcus and his white girl looked at each other before busting out in laughter.

"Oh no baby, she just know what I like, that's why I keep her around."

"My name's not white girl it, it's Kim."

Dia felt real stupid as Marcus in his white girl gangbanged. It crowded her thoughts with unnatural thing like this ménage a trios, she was about to partake in.

"First of all Dia, I want to show you that life can be totally exciting if your willing to let go of the stick you have stuck up your ass, get my drift. Just learn to go with it and let go of all the doubts your feeling right now, because I know exactly what your feeling, am I right?" Marcus asked, as he straightened the bed off so the ladies could take their places in it. Kim immediately started to undress. She knew what Marcus wanted, after all that was a part of the fantasy. To have his women ready to fuck when ever he wanted to fuck and if Dia wasn't ready to fly right, she would have to flee.

"Come on Dia, there nothing to be afraid of." Dia looked at Kim and rolled her eyes. She couldn't believe she agreed to this. But if fate would grant her wishes to get Marcus back and if this is what it took to get him back, then she was willing to try it out and see what the result would bring. She saw enough porno movies to know how white girls fucked and Dia knew if she planned on taking Marcus home with her, she better had out performed his new ho. Dia stood there disrobing. As her clothes fell to the floor, Kim made a motion as if she was waiting for Dia to hurry up and get into the bed.

"I can't wait to fuck you." Kim said to Dia.

Dia changed her mind that quick. She picked her clothes off the floor.

"Hey baby what are you doing, don't tell me you changed your mind. You'll have to excuse Kim, she's just hot that all." Marcus said, as he laid there in bed beside Kim waiting for Dia to get into bed.

"I don't think I can go through with this. I'm not Ménage trio's material."
Dia explained, as she stepped back into her panties.

Kim got off the bed walking over to Dia to get her to loosen up.

"I got you baby." She said as she took Dia's arm and took her hand slowly walking over to the bed. Before Dia could say a word Kim took both her lily white hands pulling Dia's face toward hers. She kissed her on the mouth softly. Dia eyes popped open, for she never had been kissed by a woman before. Marcus laid there watching the lived porno movie take place right in the front of his eyes. He knew in a matter of minutes Dia would be a full blown bitch, because Kim was skilled in turning a bitch out.

"That feels good don't it?" Kim said, as Dia and the kissing got more intense.

"I can't wait any longer, ya'll two ho's come on and get in this bed." Marcus said. Dia popped from under the hypnotic spell Kim had put on her.

"Who are you calling a ho."

"Don't mind him, he's just horny that's all." Kim said, as she slowly pulled Dia onto the bed. Dia couldn't believe what was happening to her, but it felt good and she didn't feel her self pulling away. But walking into what ever it was Kim and Marcus was doing to her and her feelings, making her body mclt in the palms of this white girl hands.

"I want you on top and you sucking me." Marcus said, as Kim pulled the blanket off the bed and threw it on the floor so that her and Dia could break buck wild. But Dia wasn't making an attempt to do what Marcus made clear what he wanted.

"I said I want you sucking me and you on top." Marcus said again.

Kim did exactly what he said. She saddled her self on top of Marcus while pulling Dia by the arm towards her mouth while she rode. She wanted to kiss Dia on the mouth, and Dia complied. Marcus moaned as he watched and participated in the ménage a trios he wanted. He looked deeply into Dia's eyes as Kim rode his dick. Dia looked back before she turned her head. She wasn't about to lick him after he admitted he was having sex with more than one partner. Dia finally gave in slowly but surely. The ménage a trios turned into a sexual escapade with uninitiated feeling being unleashed. The sweat poured off each participant's body, while Dia watched on as Kim gave Marcus a blow job right in front of her face, this set off deep feelings deep inside her heart. Then she remembered how her mother use to tell her that one night of sex could turn into a life time of let downs. The sex Kim gave Marcus was so good it turned into a full blown orgasm, like the drink she drank at Club

Compound just hour's earlier. As Marcus and Kim screwed Dia picked up the blanket off the floor and wiped the sweat from off of her chest. She picked up her clothes as a tear rolled down her cheek as she watched Kim take complete control of Marcus body and his emotions.

Dia made her move towards the hotel room door only to be stop dead in her tracks. Marcus popped up off the bed as the sweat rolled down his face and chest, with his legs and arms he pushed Kim off of his body like a trailer park ho that she was. Making his way across the room to block Dia before she left him for good.

"What's wrong? And where are you going?" Marcus yelled before her body stepped out into the hallway.

Move out of my way dog." Dia said as she shrugged her shoulders.

Dia took her fist, balled them up before she slammed Marcus in his chest until he took both her skinny arms in his big hands practically dragging her over to the bed.

"What the fuck are you doing to me?" She yelled back in his ears.

Kim stood there in shock before picking up the white sheet off the floor tying it in a knot in the front of her body. She leaned against the bathroom door becoming an instant accessory to a crime. She had no idea what was going to take place. Marcus picked up another white sheet ripping it from corner to corner before parting Dia's legs tying them too the corners of the four poster bed she laid in, then he took her hands doing them the exact same way.

"Look in the draw and get the duck tape," He told Kim.

Kim said "What." Just as surprised as Dia was at what their ménage a trios had turned into a serious unfortunate event.

"What the hell are you doing, Marcus?" Kim asked.

"You'll see, just go sit down so I can think." Marcus yelled in an angry voice, Kim could see he was serious as a heart attack.

"I'm getting the fuck out of here, I don't want to be down with this shit here." Kim said, as she threw the sheet she had wrapped around her body to the floor to retrieve her clothes. Dia didn't understand what was taking place, but she did do everything in her power to be set free. She wiggled, pushed with what little bit of strenght she had to push with and she twisted and turned to unloose the sheet that kept her bound.

"I got plans for you bitch." Marcus said as he climbed on top of Dia shoving his penis deep inside of her vagina. She couldn't even scream because the tape was so tightly wrapped around her mouth. Kim snuck out of the door as Marcus released himself inside of her.

"Um, Um." Dia moaned.

"Be quite ho." Marcus said in return. "I knew you would want to be down with this ménage a trios, because you ain't nothing but a nasty ass jump off. Marcus shouted to the top of his lungs, knowing Dia's mouth was covered with duck tape and he wouldn't have to worry about feed back.

"This here baby is just the beginning."

Dia seen a crazed look in Marcus eyes like she had never seen before, the look reminded her of the night she tried so hard to forget. This being the night Rod and a couple of his homeboys raped her, leaving her with the marks deep inside of her being to prove it.

CHAPTER 17

Destini listened as the entourage of cars pulled off leaving skid marks as they turned the corner with Boo's body still in the trunk headed to Meachy's house. Once they arrived Sham commanded his youngest soldier remove Boo from the trunk in nothing but a pair of boxer shorts. He dragged Boo's body through Meachy house to his office where he sat. The soldier knocked on the door happy to have the thief right there in his possession. He would be willing to carry out what ever forms of torture Meachy commanded. After all he was the boss of bosses in the ATL and what ever he said went, no questions asked.

"Come in." Meachy yelled as he sat at his big oak wood desk twirling his thumbs.

"We got him Meachy." The youngest soldier in the squad said as he pushed Boo's body to the floor like a wet dish rag.

Meachy stood there with an angry look on his face. To him there wasn't nothing worst on god's green earth then a thief in Meachy's eyes. He planned on torturing Boo for taking something that didn't belong to him, especially his shit. Meachy got out of his seat and walked around his desk kicking Boo in the rib cage.

"So you're the bold one I keep hearing about, huh." He said as he commanded his youngest soldier to pick Boo up and sit his limp body in the chair.

"I never stole anything from you, man. Somebody's trying to pen this crime on me."

"So where exactly did this come from, if it's not mine mother fucker? You fit the description of the nigga that came into one of my trap houses on the BLVD, stealing from me and threatening my lieutenants."

"It wasn't me man, I never seen that stack of money before." Boo yelled trying to defend himself like an attorney. Meachy threw the neatly stacked money on his hard wood desk and stood in the front of Boo with his arms folded and legs crossed ready to give orders of execution.

"Now I'm going to ask you this, why did you pick my trap house to rob? Why? You think your invisible mother fucker. The whole town knows you been the one hitting up trap houses for a very long time now, but this time you picked the wrong mother fucking trap house to fuck wit." Meachy used his hand creating a hand signal, only him and his squad could identify. Signaling for the young soldier that he was about to promote to a lieutenant to come a little closer.

When Boo lied to Meachy he signed his own death certificate. The soldier grabbed Boo's arms pulling him out of his seat to take him to the back, to a specially padded room sound proof to any outsiders. Boo was quickly blind folded and pushed against the padded wall. There was nothing left to say at this point, but some how he blurted out his last words.

"Fuck you. That's why you'll never see the rest of your money." Boo screamed before he stuck up his middle finger. Meachy commanded to get the thief out of his sight.

Sham stood there looking quit angry, before he bowed his head. Twelve guns were brought onto the scene. Glocks, Smith & Westons, and a saw off shot gun and a variety of other weapons. Each man stood at attention before they all held their guns up at the same time, pumping holes all over Boo's body. His lifeless body fell to the floor covered with plastic. The plastic was wrapped around Boo's body and the body transported to another location where the clean up crew would clean up the mess that Boo created for himself. The plastic was unwrapped and the body dumped into a tub of acid that would finally dissolve Meachy's and Destini's big problem, Boo.

After the elimination process Meachy commended his squad for a job well done. After the smiles and laughing, another meeting came to the surface. He sat each one down to give them explicit details of the next hit. That's being K-Killer. He sat down for a minute to take a deep breath. He thought before he breathed out any more directions, being a leader with power was a big job whether anybody knew it or not.

"The next job will take place in Miami. So I want you, you and you to carry this one out."

Meachy pointed to the youngest soldier that had just been penned with honors to go out on his second hit. Meachy also commanded Sham to go with him, and take with him lots of artillery.

"Where exactly does this next nigga live?" Sham asked, eager to get the show on the road so he could get back to Atlanta.

"He lives in Miami in a Spanish Villa on the beach, here's the address." Meachy hand the piece of paper to Sham.

"He's creating a whole lot of problems in the community," Meachy said. Sham shuck his head, for he knew at this point Dolorian had fucked Meachy and had his head in the same cloud his was in. He held his head down, for he thought Meachy was slipping.

"I know you're not talking about?" Before the words could come all the way out of Sham's mouth, Meachy gave him a real dirty look. Sham quickly closed his mouth, for he knew the spell, pussy could do to the brain and if Meachy got off on the feeling then so be it.

The cars were gassed up and Sham rode in his Hummer with the gold rims. His job wasn't at all hard for a nigga clocking six digits at the end of each year. Sham would pack his shit and hit the big apple, he sat there as he drove thinking about some of the honeys he left behind and the honeys he planned on sleeping with, before the new year hit. His mind was very well schooled on the feeling and what it could do to you. His mother always told him when he was coming up, never get a girl pregnant until he found a job and was able to support his seed. He was feeling

Meachy. His mind flashed back to the exotic dance Dolorian did for him while she was trying to make a point about getting her ex whacked. His flash back took him to the very beginning when Dolorian stepped out of her Gucci outfit and revealed her laced thong to him. He loved it but was too tough to admit it. After all a thug wasn't supposed to let a woman know when he was in too deep, that would make him look like a pussy whipped chump and he wasn't about to let this happen.

Sham thought about it and how he wanted to try her out just one more time when he returned to Atlanta. She had to have something else sexual up her sleeve for her to pull the boss of bosses and have his head in the clouds like she had Meachy's. Sham and his entourage of cars cruised down to Miami Beach to carry out a hit on K-Killa. He cruised along the Pacific looking at the beautiful beaches something that he didn't see much the ATL. The sun popped out of the sky making things look much clearer to his eyes. K-Killa's house came into view, he called each one of his men on their cell phone to let them know that the house was in eye view and that before they made a move things would have to be planned out carefully.

"They Park around the corner." He commanded as the entourage to pulled up around the corner. A baby blue Q pulled into K-Killa drive way. As Sham sat there on the corner of the house, he could see K-Killa wife step out of the car with her child by the hand.

"I see a female, she just stepped inside of the house." Sham said letting his squad know what was going on, so that he could tell them exactly how he planned on moving.

"So what do you suggest we do?" The youngest in the squad asked.

"You tell me what you think we should do? after all you're the one who received an honor today. What would you do in a situation like this one?" Sham asked the youngest squad member.

"Do you really want to know what I'd do in a situation like this?" He asked Sham.

"Yeah, young playa. What would you do?" Sham asked laughing, trying to kill time since it was still light outside.

"Me my self, I would go in there and just blast everything in sight." The young soldier said thinking about all the mob movie he had seen in his eighteen years of life.

"Oh hell no, we do handle shit like that. This is not ABC or CBS, we handle things in a more sophisticated way young playa. This is how it will be done. As soon as the sun goes all the way down, we're going to go in there and drag his ass out of bed. Just like we did the other nigga, But you see there is a difference in the situations. This person we was sent here to take out is a community problem. His problem is not that of being a thief, his is with his dick. He slung his dick in the wrong direction and has created a problem with his way of slinging.

"Now what do you suggest we do to him young soldier?" Sham asked once again, to see if the answer would sound human this time.

"Chop that mother fuckers Johnson off," the soldier said.

Sham fell out laughing, for he seen this answer coming before the soldier spit it out. He was crouched to the side laughing until he seen a jet black hummer truck just like his, fly out of K-Killa drive way.

"We're on alert." Sham said before all the cars started their engine trying to catch up.

K-Killa had no idea who these nigga was that was trailing along behind his hummer. He sped through the streets headed out to go on his sexual sight tour in his neighborhood in Miami Florida. He was searching for a Cuban honey to kick it with for the evening, leaving his wife and child at home to worry about his whereabouts. His dick was on call and no family could stop that. This was all a part of being a sex addict and a part of being high. Looking, wanting and needing. This was the cravings he felt inside of his being on the regular. Pussy called him out of his bed in the morning, evening, noon and at night. There wasn't a corner of Miami beach that he wasn't going to comb, looking for the piece of ass he craved.

He looked through his rearview mirror as Sham's hummer trailed along beside his. Sham blew the horn to let him know it was on.

"Who in the hell are these fools?" K-Killa asked himself, as his hummer did all 120 miles per hour, trying to get away. Just as he tried to switch lanes, a cop car sped behind him turning on it's cherry top lights to let K-Killa know to pull over to the side and stay his black ass inside of his car. K-Killa ignored the call and kept going. Sham's hummer slowed down along with all the other vehicles that were traveling with him. Sham laughed as he seen the cop car trail along beside K-Killa hummer before K-Killa turned the corner. As he did, ten more cop cars were called in on a wild high speed chase. He kept going scared to stop, considering he had a pound of weed in the glove compartment. Sham kept behind the cops and K-killa, waiting to see the results of the high speed chase.

"This is some OJ shit happening right here in front of our eyes." Sham said to himself. He hoped the cops would take care of his light work before he would have to. He'd rather be some where eating a dancers pussy instead of being in the middle of Miami beach chasing a sex addict who was a community problem in Meachy's eyes.

The cop cars finally corner K-Killa. He tried to get a way, but they just wouldn't let him. Before K-Killa could stop his car good, they had him cornered. One of the cops stepped out of his car with the bull horn he had in his hand. K-Killa's car door opened, Meachy's crew parked down the block just like half of the Miami resident, trying to see the out come of a nigga gone kamikaze just like OJ did, his leg came out of the car.

"Sir, remain in the car and put your hands up where we can see them." The cop yelled through the bull horn.

K-Killa ignored the warning and put one foot outside of the car. As soon as it hit the pavement you could hear the click of the police guns. The view was pleasant to Sham and his crew. To actually watch the cops take down one of their jobs, was brilliant. He would be able to ride all the way back to Atlanta with a clear conscious, for once in his life.

"I want you to step out of the car with both hands in the air." The cop yelled through the bull horn, creating a crowd of cars all around them. The Florida residence wanted to know what was going on in the middle of the expressway and the news team was called in, from all the excitement that took place with the O.J. high speed chase.

"Did you bring some popcorn Sham?" Rosco asked, as he laughed, practically falling-out of his seat.

"No. But now I wish I did." Sham said, responding.

"This shit is better than the Friday night movies. Look at this dumb mother fucker, that's what he get for making us use so much fucking gas following his dumb ass," Rosco said.

"Yeah man. I figured the shit would end sooner or later, look." Sham said, as he kept his eyes on the target while talking on his cell phone to Rosco.

He seen all ten cops plus the extra cops that pulled up for back up. They all made an attempt to go towards K-Killa, ready to take the predator down if he made the wrong move. This was a do or die situation in the eyes of the law.

"Hold up man." K-KIlla yelled to the cops, as he went to dig in his pockets. As he did the guns went off like a salute on Veterans Day. His body hit the ground. As soon as it did Meachy was called.

"Guess what man, the police just shot this fool in the middle of the expressway." Sham said before him and his entourage turned their cars around headed back home to the ATL.

"Good, come on home boy's." Meachy said before he hung up his phone. He didn't need to hear any more. That was enough to penetrate his ears. He called Dolorian to let her knew her problem had been eliminate and that he wanted her to stop by his house when ever she got the chance. Dolorian was happy, she could return home now. The fear of being killed or hurt by K-Killa was over, even though he was the last thing on her mind. She still feared being hurt, for trying to kill him with the gamma.

CHAPTER 18

Marcus was past mad. He sat in a chair by the bed trying to figure out exactly what drove him to this point. Then he thought about what would happen if he decided to let Dia go and how she would be so mad she would definitely get him locked up. She laid there unable to talk for the duck tape was still over her mouth. She just wonder exactly what it was that Marcus planned on doing to her after all the years of faithful service she provided for him, since he was her lover for years and now this. What exactly was it that made a woman fed up with the bullshit men put them through. Dia thought to herself. Was her man bugging out after all, she wanted him back and he knew this but yet he wanted to make an already fucked up situation worst.

"I know exactly what we're going to do, I'm having a couple of my boys over like I did with you once before. You know that night you surprised me with your freaky behavior, remember?" Marcus said as he still had the crazed look in his eyes. All Dia could do was lay there and let him do what ever his imagination told him to do. She knew at this point Marcus had a serious problem, one she had read about before becoming a teacher. She was exposed to a lot of literature and she also read a lot like most teacher did and then she remembered an article she read explaining the problem that is big in our society, but not many people care or even notice. She used her scientific thinking to put together pieces to a puzzle that was embezzled in her mind. Marcus was definitely a sexual predator, he used fetishes to get him in. When all he really cared about was his own black ass, nothing else mattered. Nobodies feelings, nobodies love. Just the feeling he had cared about. She remembered the word paraphilia and how a paraphlia was considered psycho if the scientist told the story.

It was like he always got off on hurting her and she was sick and tired of her feeling being ignored and wanted revenge now like Dolorian suggested before she told her to loose her phone number.

"I got a couple of the boy's lined up for tonight in case you're wondering." Marcus made clear one last time.

Dia twist her body from side to side trying hard to roll, but the torn sheet prevented her from doing so.

"Are you trying to tell me something?" Marcus asked as he smiled, still looking crazy.

Dia moaned since she couldn't say much of anything else.

"I'll tell you what since you been cooperating with me to the fullest extent, I'm going to undo the tape and when I do if you even think about screaming I'll kill you." Marcus said before showing her he meant business.

He undid the tape.

"Please let me go Marcus." Dia asked still turning her body from side to side.

"Shut up." Marcus yelled before he balled up his fist.

"Why are you doing this to me Marcus?" Dia asked, still moving around from side to side.

"If you cooperate I'll undo the sheets that got your ass bind to that head board." Marcus looked serious, so Dia took it as that. She refused to tick off an already ticking time bomb. Marcus let it be known that he was out to kill, if she made the wrong move and he meant each and every word that spilled out of his mouth. Dia knew he would, just like he changed up on her in Rod's basement in front of his crew of sucker friends.

"Why are you treating me this way Marcus, all I ever tried to do was love you and this is the love you felt for me all of the years we were together. Why didn't you tell me, if you would have I wouldn't be sitting here in your face right now, Is there anyway we can rectify this right now and make shit right, huh?" Dia poured out the feeling she felt right then and Marcus listened in, but didn't comprehend at all what she was trying to say. He acted as if his mind was in a whole nother zone, like it had been in for years even when he laid in her bed every night making love to her.

"How is it you can even say this to me after you fucked Rod right in front of my face bitch."

"I thought you said you forgave me for that. Now you are bringing that ole shit up again. Come on now that's the reason I called you, because I knew time went by and I thought you might had forgiven me by now. But damn! If I knew you felt that way about me and that you would have to lure me to a hotel room to make your self look good in front of the white girl you're shacking up with. She's gone so just let it go and let me go Marcus." Dia speech went on for a long time but Marcus still didn't want to hear nothing she said, all he could see in the back of his mind was his best friend pumping his dick further and further in his woman and she let him. This was all that was on his mind.

"Listen Dia, nothing you say means nothing to me any more. You screwed over me and I let you."

"Screwed over you how about me Marcus, how do you think I feel about the way you screwed over me? Why do you think I asked you to come join me at Club Compound for drinks, to hurt you or to try to love you, answer me this one question?" Dia asked, with the look of love still in her eyes even after Marcus degraded her as a woman once again.

"I think you get off on me hurting you. Look at you, still begging me to come back to you. Can't you see I don't want you." Marcus said holding his head down.

Dia cried, wondering how could somebody who was born with a heart like his be so damn cold and empty.

"Yeah, your right I been a true fool to even waste my time caring about you even when you called me a slut after Rod raped me." Dia crying became intense

"I could have called the police in on the situation and have you and your boys locked up, but I didn't like a fool. I went on loving you and I still can't believe I still love you Marcus after all the shit you've put me through."

Instead of Marcus turning to Dia supporting her for loving him he turned the other cheek.

"Let me go Marcus please. I can't take much more from you, my heart is already broken and now you want to just step on it until you draw blood."

"I hate you and don't think I'm capable of ever loving you again, as a matter of fact I never loved you." Marcus toughness began to shine through, his toughness against love and the feelings of love. This was not in his thugged out vocabulary. Dia was sounding insane to him. Kim never said I love you, she just put up with what ever Marcus wanted to do, and what ever Marcus wanted whether sexual or not. In other words, Kim was down for what ever. What thugs call the round the way girls, this was Kim.

"How can you stand there and call your self a man after all I've done for you. I shared you with bitches every since you came into my life and this is the respect I get from you. Marcus you're a dirty mother fucking low down dog." Dia screamed before Marcus ran over to the duck tape and slapped another piece over her mouth, once Dia started screaming. Marcus explained that he had his boys coming over again for a special reunion. Dia cried and as the tears rolled down her face, there was nothing she could do. Marcus got dressed and left the hotel room headed to the lobby of Hotel Twelve, just as he stepped off the elevator Dolorian spotted him with her special radar that seemed to zero in on one of her girls men. She never seemed to miss a trick.

"Marcus what's up baby?" She yelled across the hotel lobby generating an audience.

Marcus cringed, he couldn't believe Dolorian was checking into the hotel where he had Dia tied to the head board with duck tape over her mouth.

"How's Dia?" Dolorian asked waiting for a response to see if he and she were back together. Like Boo and Destini backstabbed her in the back, by clicking off with each other once again. She had a flashback of Destini and Boo going into Café Dupri's together into the VIP lounge where every nigga in Georgia loved to hang out and eat. Before she could pull herself out of the daydream state, Marcus started to walk off.

Dolorian could see he was still a shiesty character like he always been and then she remember how she hated him from the get go and then Dolorian noticed how Marcus was the only one still hanging around. She hadn't a clue Boo met his maker at the end of a barrel of a shot gun, a glock, and a variety of other heavy artillery. Dolorian always wanted to know what was up with him and Dia. She decided to get into her candy apple red BMW and follow him through the streets of ATL. She watched as Marcus pulled into the driveway of the Westin Hotel and let a valet take control of his car. She waited until he reached for the hotel door to open it before she hopped out of her car and slowly trailed behind him. She entered the hotel and noticed him at the elevator. She just sat there in the lobby until he came back down, but when he did he had a white gentleman with him. The man was dressed in a suit like a business men wear. The conversation between him and Marcus was flowing, the man acted as if he knew Marcus for years.

Dolorian didn't want to be spotted, Just like she didn't want to be spotted when she ran into him in the past, at Peppers Bar and Grill. Marcus hadn't a clue Dolorian was so interested in him. He wouldn't even image her following him, like an ole hound dog fresh on his tracks. What Marcus was doing, looked to Dolorian like he was making some sort of deal with this man he walked with. Dolorian wanted to hear what was being said,like a fly on the wall. Marcus finally shack the white man's hand and walked back out to the hotel valet, to retrieve his keys to his car.

"Damn." Dolorian said to herself as she ran behind a valet to get her keys too.

The valet ran to get Dolorian's car as she rushed him to do so. She gave him a five dollar tip and took off trying to play catch up. She wasn't about to let the nigga that raped her best friend just ride off into the sunset. She felt as if she was the Bella mafia bitch, especially after fucking Meachy. This made shit feel real officiall, like she always wanted it to be all of her life. That's one of the reasons she took the job as a dancer, to attract the type of men all female desired One who was totally in control, and called all the shot. In other words, a shot calling nigga with a big black dick, slinging it like he was Tarzan and her name was Jane. Dolorian became extremely nosey, she followed Marcus straight through the streets of Atlanta Georgia and down some country rode. There was no deferring her and she meant business. She thought about how her friend was blind, if she even considered going back to such a dog of Marcus character. The streets he hit up were quit dark but Dolorian continued to follow Marcus's lead. He drove out to where the house was, big as tow mansions. Dolorian [parked on the corner to watch, was he going into a female's house but he didn't. The door opened as an Italian man stepped out. He had a cigar hanging from the brim of his big lips. Marcus moved in real close with this gentleman as if he was still making deals.

After hours of waiting, Dolorian followed Marcus. He ended back at the hotel. Dolorian would not let dead dogs lie. She checked back into the hotel. She ran over to the desk clerk and pointed to Marcus as he stepped on the elevator.

"I want a room on the same floor my cheating husband is on." The desk clerk looked at her for spicing up her evening. She knew Marcus from the many trips him and his white girl made, going in and out of the hotel on numerous occasions.

"That's your husband?" The young girl working the desk asked.

"Yes, I know he's cheating on me that's why I'm following him."

"He's on the third floor ma'am." The girl answered

"Oh really." Dolorian answered back.

The desk clerk moved in a little closer before busting Dolorian's bubble.

"He's shacked up there with a white girl and a guess. I saw the white girl storming out of here when I came on my shift. I'm working a double so I got to see him last night. He also took a black girl up there with him and the white girl late last night. They were all hugged up on each other." The desk clerk disclosed.

Dolorian eyes blew up wide as quarter this was some juicy gossip coming across her ears.

"I' don't know what's going on up there but I hear it real freaky. One of the guess, that has a room next door said there's a lot of sex going on in that man's room. Not to mention he was arguing with somebody up there not to long ago."

"Damn, you know all this. You're good." Dolorian gave the desk clerk a hand shake for she knew she would be on Marcus trail most definitely. She retrieved her key card and knew she had to know if the female in the room with him was Dia or one of his many ho's that she and all Dia friends knew he was screwing on the side. The mistery was worth trying to find out and get to the bottom of it.

When A Woman's Fed Up

CHAPTER 19

Marcus's room on the third floor just so happened to be next door to a vacant room. Dolorian took it, once the desk clerk gave her the run down of how the tenant that once lived there moved into a bigger place, since a job promotion she waited came through. Room three hundred had been vacant for at least a month and she offered it to her. Dolorian practically grabbed the key card out of the desk clerks hand. Her intuition told her she was doing the right thing and all for a good cause. Most women had intuition, especially when it came down to a no good man like Marcus, K-Killa and Wallace. God obviously broke the mold when he created these characters.

Dolorian never once considered K-Killa accidental death was at the hands of Miami Florida's notorious Police Department. This made what she was trying to do look like a piece of cake considering. Which in all nationality was to commit murder. She rode the elevator up to her newly assigned room which was located right next door to Marcus room. She hoped to bust his black ass wide open. So that her friend Dia could see what a dog he really was, and maybe just maybe, she'd ask her to be her sista and best friend like they had been for years.

"I can't believe my girl's dog is so damn dirty." Dolorian said, as she stepped foot in her room and closed the door quickly behind her hoping Marcus wouldn't get wind that she was his next door neighbor. She sat her Gucci duffle bags in a dark corner. She never once planned on staying. She just wanted to know why would her girl's even consider wanting their men back. She didn't want to see them all make the same mistakes as she did when she let K-Killa in, breaking down mental barriers that she barricaded between her self and the male population. Sakina's problem was the first of their problems that practically took care of it self, with Wallace practically taking himself out with his unforgivable sexual behaviors and appetites. Dolorian had some undisclosed issues in her life just as well, that all demanded immediate attention. Yet she always insisted on putting her girl friends first in foremost. This whole fucked up situation seemed like a night mare. One day planning revenge plots and months later actually carrying these twisted thoughts out to the fullest extent. Like the ole heads always told her when they would come to see her on stage, shaking her ass. Easy comes the good times and easy goes the good times. Dolorian planted her ear on the ice cold wall trying to investigate for herself what the desk clerk gossiped to her about, to see if it rang true. All she heard in the distance of Marcus room was the sounds of muffled out talking. She noticed she definitely was in the wrong spot. So she moved her undercover operation into another part of her hotel room. This was one of the reasons she loved the Hotel Twelve, their walls there were paper thin. She could zero in a little closer placing her ear on the kitchen wall hoping for a closer range of listening pleasure, only to get more disappointed. She wanted to know each phone call he made and everybody who came to his room's name, to find out if her best girl friend got back with her no good ass man.

She pressed her ear even harder to the wall until the lobe turned beet red. She wanted to know so desperately what kind of business deals Marcus was involved in, like he was her man or something. Her heart felt as if it would burst wide open from all the excitement and the fact that she was keeping it all to herself. She slipped her cell phone out of its holster before scrolling down the menu of names and close friends and contacts. This is when she came across Dia's number. Dolorian knew at this moment that Dia was more than a best friend, she was like a sista to her, one who shared ideas. One who shared advice and one who made her laugh at times when Dolorian tried playing hard from time to time. Dolorian thought about this before she pushed the button to dial Dia's number. When she finally did the phone rang. It rang continuously as she still had her ear pressed up against the wall. She could hear the phone ring in Marcus room she whispered.

"Pick it up nigga."

With her cell phone on one ear and one ear pressed up against the wall, there was no doubt before the day or night was out she would definitely hear something.

"Shit." Marcus said, before he physically picked the phone up and threw it across the room smashing it to pieces. Just as he did there was a knock on the hotel room door.

"Who is it," Marcus yelled.

"Danny." The man said as he waited patiently to be let in.

Dolorian had a feeling some action was about to take place, finally she propped her ass up on the toilet seat with her ear still pressed up against the wall.

"So this is the girl Danny said," his voice was so heavy it penetrated Dolorian's ear drums.

"Where is the white girl you had here before. I'd rather have both of them if you don't mind?"

"She's not here, but I promise that the next time I'll make sure I bring that to life for you, but for right now this is it."

"Sure, sure no problem she'll do me just fine. Danny said.

"Damn, what the hell do Marcus got going on over there?" Dolorian said to herself, all she could hear at this point was a bed rocking and it's head board crashing against the wall over and over again.

"Wow." Dolorian said, as her heart raced just from observing on the opposite side of the wall. When the man finished his manly duties, she could hear him breathing heavily. But not one time did she hear a woman groan, moan or even sigh or make any kind of noise, like women do. When the bed squeak to the point that the bed sound like it would break in half or no body saying fuck me's, she heard nothing.

Dolorian came to the conclusion that Marcus was fucking this man on the DL, then she thought about all the juicy gossip the desk clerk fed her.

"Nah, aint no way."

Dolorian stuck her ear back to the wall. This time she could hear as the door slammed. When Marcus returned to the room, she could hear as the man paid Marcus for the best time of his life with a mute partner. Then they both laughed as Dia laid there in shock at the situation. She caught in-between without any help what so ever. When one man left another one arrived not ten minute behind the first as if he was running some kid of game next door.

"I thought you said she'd be able to do me like I described to you. How is that possible with her tied up like that." The man asked. Dolorian could tell this one was white by the tone of his voice.

"She can man she can, and if you have another fantasy she can bring that one to life too. There is nothing she can't do, it's just going to cost you a little bit more."

Dolorain said "What." Before she opened her phone and tried to dial her best friend's number once again and this time if she didn't answer, Dolorian decided to look into this matter herself.

"I'm willing to pay you top dollar, if she can do what I ask you too. When you approached me on the streets." The white man said.

"No problem man." Marcus said trying to make his customer more comfortable.

"Well then, how much is it for a fellatio job." The white man asked.

"What man?" Marcus asked. He wasn't use to hearing men call a blow job a fellatio job. This was definitely white terminology for getting your dick blew off.

Dolorian knew Marcus was up to no good, at this point she dialed Dia's number one last time, but still there was no answer. She put the phone down one last time to continue to listen in on the fellatio job going on next door to her room. Marcus voice appeared to be getting louder but he wasn't hollering at the man. He appeared to be yelling at a woman.

"If you scream when I take the tape off, I'll kill you." He said angrily to Dia. Dolorian had no idea he was yelling at her best friend and sista. Dia's body was stretched out on the bed and her eyes were filled with tears and her heart with pain of betrayal, from the man she thought she was deeply in love with. Marcus had truly out did himself this time, making her have sexual relations with all those strange men he brought into his hotel room from off the side walks of Atlanta, Georgia. She was now a captive with no way out and a real sure fire money maker, if Marcus told the story

Men came from all parts of town and some from out of town to his hotel room, all day and night long. Making her do things to them she had never heard of before and Marcus the man she shared her bed with for years, sat back and let them do what ever to his ex. This was his way of taking out revenge for all the things he thought to be fucked up in their relationship when they had one. She would never be able to find a spot in her heart to forgive him this time. The men he brought in made her give them blow jobs, anal sex. Some just wanted their penis's stimulated with her mouth and tongue. The whole game Marcus played with her life became quit ugly.

"Since you haven't screamed for help, that's a plus in your corner." Marcus said, as if he was doing her a favor.

"What?" Dia asked, weak from being push, pulled, and penetrated all night long and half the day.

Marcus was so cruel he wouldn't let her finish her sentence. He slapped a piece of tape over her mouth once again,

"You see, men love it when they can get the pussy with no strings attached to it. I'm going to make shit easier for you here, take this."

Marcus pulled out a package that contained a light green substance it appeared to be in powder form.

"This here is Spanish fly, it's guaranteed to get you in the mood." He opened the substance and slipped it into a bottle of Pepsi. Pulling the tape off of her mouth he forced her to drink it.

"I have a couple of super freaks I want you to meet to day." Marcus said, and Dia's eyes got big as a quarter, since it was impossible for her to do much with tape over her mouth.

"One he just wants a Roman Shower, and the other wants a Golden shower. Do you know what this is?" He asked as if she could answer.

Dia held her head down while shaking it no. She wished what ever was wrong with Marcus would be cured.

"Well a roman shower means he wants you to shit on him, that's something you seem to be good at just like you shit on me and my world, remember? And the other guy, he just wants you to piss in his face, and check this out the fellows a cop." Marcus became tickled pink to know he could actually bring a cop into his hotel room for sex and not get arrested.

"I'll tell you this baby, this world is definitely filled with super freaks. Sex has definitely turned some of these mother fuckers out." Marcus revealed.

Dia knew her life as she knew it was completely over. She knew her students she taught would be worried about her, and now she found her self tied down unable to use her mobility to break free from the man she once loved, but now hated. She wondered did she drive Marcus crazy that night in Rod's basement or did he go crazy afterwards. Dolorian heard each and every rotten word that spilled off his lips. She wished she could rip his tongue out. She knew who ever the female that was being abused definitely was catching hell next door. Dolorian never like Marcus and planned on going up in his room as soon as he left it, to see who this poor woman was. She knew this was a man that had no respect for the female gender and would do what ever, just because he was an abuse child.

Marcus took the tape off one last time to make Dia drink the aphrodisiac, he put in her drink. This time she would try to call out for help.

"Please let me go Marcus, let me go. Stop what your doing to me. What have I done to you to make you treat me this way"

Dolorian listened in to the female voice and the sounds sounded familiar to her, but she just couldn't put her finger on who it belong to. This really made her heart race, just wanting to know who it was and she vowed she'd find out.

CHAPTER 20

Meachy was concerned about Dolorian, considering she hadn't been in touch since the hit she put out on K-Killa, that just so happened to turn into a spectacle, thanks to the Miami Police Department. He dialed her number to see exactly what was going on with her and wanted to see her on his leisure time. He was a gangsta, but usually his leisure time dealt with playing a good ole fashion game of golf. There was definitely no woman he couldn't pull, no not one. He had what all woman wanted and was surprised that Dolorian wasn't calling like some woman would had by now. He sent a car by her home to see if she was alright. When the car returned, the driver told Meachy, Dolorian was no where to be found. He had no idea Dolorian was at Hotel Twelve. She hadn't called since her little lap dance episode.

Dolorian imagination got the best of her. She wouldn't even pick up her cell phone to answer Meachy's call. She was dead set on finding out what was going on in room 301. Dia laid there wondering why was Marcus bursting into the hotel room like he was on fire. He had a big black bag in his hand. When he went to reach inside of it he pulled out a big blue dildo, Dia thought she would faint. He ran over towards her and started to strap the device to her privates, as if he had gone completely insane. He untied her hands first, then her feet. Making her get down on all fours by force, in the middle of the bed. Then he tied a black neck tie around her eyes, making it impossible for her to see what her next quest was. Just as he did, there was a soft knock at the door with a feminine appeal.

"Come on in its open." Marcus yelled.

Dolorian couldn't change positions fast enough, from one position to the next.

"Damn, when you said bondage you meant bondage. The purple head pump rocker said when she stepped into the room. She closed the door behind her before she started to undress. Dia became totally restless, for she hadn't a clue what was about to take place this time to her sexually. She could see that Marcus was trying to mold her into something that she was not and she had no choice but to lay there and pray and not bend to Marcus will he tried to impose on her.

"I'm ready man, I've already paid you remember?" The female said, as she took to the bed.

She snatched the dildo off of Dia and strapped it to herself, before forcefully breaking Dia a brand new ass hole. Dia's mouth was bound so tight her screams turned into chokes by ricocheting backwards. Marcus was amazed at what wonders a female could perform, once given the opportunity and the proper equipment. He watched as the strapped female gripped her hands around Dia's hips and thrust the fake penis inside her until Dia's body looked as if the spirit had gone right out of her. When the female rapist finished, she had to check and see if Dia was still alive. Marcus let his last patronizing customer out of his hotel room, before locking the door and throwing each and every dime he made on the bed,while he had his ex woman tied up and bound with no way of getting away or loose. He counted money for a good hour and a half until his black brief case was filled to the top with the large quantity of money he had collected.

"Bye bitch it's been fun." He said before taking the money and leaving Dia in the same position. Dolorian said, "Oh, no he didn't."

She cracked her hotel room door peeping out to see Marcus trail his way to the elevator with his brief case and other luggage in hand. She waited until he was gone before making a move. She tapped on door 301 before trying the door knob to ask the unknown woman did she need assistance, but the door was locked. Marcus had left Dia there tied up to die. Dolorian opened her cell phone to call down stairs commanding that the clerk come upstairs to let her inside the room, once she explained that some freaky behavior was being performed to someone inside the room. The desk clerk did a hundred yard dash to comply with Dolorian's demand. The desk clerk became nervous trying to stick the key card into the slot of the door that would trigger the lock to open, before they both burst inside to find Dia bound and gagged with her eyes blood shot red, from all the tears she had sheded while begging her maker to send her help from the sanctuary and that's exactly what he did.

"Oh my gods untie her." Dolorian yelled to the desk clerk and she did. She was shocked to find Dia tied up and bound, then she cried along with the desk clerk once they both seen an illegal abduction had taken place.

"I'll kill him." Dolorian yelled to the top of her lungs. She knew her revenge plot had turned into something real ugly, but this really took the cake.

"She's a mess look at her." The desk clerk said before bursting out into tears once again. Dolorian could see Marcus wanted to die from what he had done to one of her best friends. Meachy was the first person that popped into her mind and she planned to call him to see if he could bring another community problem to their knees where they belonged.

But first she took Dia to the bathroom and helped her get into the tub before calling the police on Marcus, for the rape that took place months ago and this. Dia could have died and if Dolorian didn't follow Marcus she would had. Dia kissed Dolorian on the cheek and told her never to leave her again. Then she tried to explain what had happened to her the best way she could, being shaken up and all. Just as the desk clerk left the room, Dolorian took Dia out of the room wrapped up in a white sheet, because Marcus had taken her clothes.

"Don't worry, Darling, I'm going to kill that mother fucker." Dolorian took Dia home and on the way out, she told the desk clerk to cancel the call she had made to the police department.

Dolorian took Dia home with her and made sure she was tucked in to bed to heal from the scares she received trying to love a man who had violated her once before

"I told you didn't I," Dolorian said.

"Yes you did and I just wouldn't listen to what you were trying to say to me. I thought I could get my man back, that's the only reason I asked him to come to Club Compound. But when he came, he showed up with a white girl on his arm. She and he ask me to come to their hotel room." Dia didn't want to disclose the information concerning being involved in a ménage a trios.

"Why would you go with him Dia? You know Marcus is shiesty, he's never to be trusted. I thought you learned this the night he let his homeboys rape you"

"Dia turned over, she was just to weak to continue talking to Dolorian.

"Don't worry I'm going to handle this, I promise you.

Dolorian knew she could count on Meachy, but just didn't want to look silly asking him to take out all the men she was angry at. So she decides to do the job her self. Since he wouldn't put a fire arm in her hands personally, she went out of the house headed to the local pawn shop where she knew she could get a gun. She enters the store in a disguise, not wanting to be seen by no one. The pawn shop owner showed her a variety of hand guns. Dolorian made her choice, and left the store confident that Marcus would be at Club Compound. where she went that night to scope the place out and saw marcus.

The crowd was thick in the club and the girls wild. She took a seat at the bar listening to the DJ spin his records, looking at each and every male face in the crowd. She spotted him with a entourage of women all around him and looked as if he was having a really good time, not caring that he had left his ex woman Dia in a hotel room strapped up bound and ready to die. Dolorian's rage swelled up inside of her. She couldn't hold back, just as she reached inside of her Prada purse she pulled the gun out and knew that she couldn't just shot him in the crowd, she would have to lure him outside.

"Marcus?" She yelled over all the loud music and the laughter of the woman he was circled by.

"Hell no." Marcus said, as he picked up his drink swatting woman out of his way to get out of the path way of Dolorian. He knew Dia's friends didn't care much for him, he just wondered why Dolorian happened to keep popping up.

"Marcus how are you baby." She said as she sat down at the bar beside him.

"He wondered could she know what he did to Dia."

Dolorian smiled showing her beautiful pearly whites to him and he smiled back showing his support.

"You know what Marcus, I always wanted to be in your company you know. How about me and you hang out, how about it?" Dolorian asked. Marcus was shocked, for he would have never imaged Dolorian wanting to be with him sexually.

"Well this is a surprise, when can we get together then?" Marcus asked.

"Now I don't think I can wait any longer how about this," Dolorian whisper sweet nothings in his ear and he smiled from all the attention.

She whispered for him to come outside. They could fuck in her BMW truck, he like it. That sounded freaky to him, being a freak in all was one of his main fortes.

Dolorian and Marcus walked hand and hand outside of Club Compound, as soon as they turned the dark corner of the parking lot, she pulled out the small caliber hand gun pointing it in his direction. She had no idea a cope car sat near by in the bush waiting for speeding cars to cross it's path.

"Hey fool, what are you doing, You need to put that away." Marcus yelled.

Dolorain told him to walk towards the car and he did, with his hands up in the air like the police was arresting him or something.

"You should have never fucked with my best friend Dia, and now you had the nerve to leave her to die in your hotel room, how you Marcus?"

Marcus smiled, he hadn't a conscious he didn't care.

"I'm going to kill you, you dirty mother fucker." Just as Dolorian picked her hand up to shoot Marcus, the cops snuck up on her from behind. Grabbed her hands and took the gun from her. She never seen it coming, Marcus of course smiled. He was set free to go and do the same dirt he did to Dia once again while Dolorain was arrested and thrown in jail without bond.

Sakina changed her life and started living it to the fullest, while Destini kept her promise to god by becoming saved and filled with the Holy Ghost. This was the promise she had made to her maker, for sparing her life from the hands of the mighty men like Meachy's squad. Dia became a rape councilor. She helped young girls identify with the rift raft in the street, by teaching them the proper procedures to save their lives, if ever put in the position that she had been put in by the man she once loved Marcus.

<u>Order this & other Bent Publishing titles</u>

_____**Do You Really Know Your Man, $15**
_____**Out Of The Game, $15**
_____**Official Contact Pages for Self Publishing, $14.95**
_____**Official Contact Pages to the Music Industry, $19.95**
_____**Official Contact Pages to the Music Industry (Dictionary), $19.95**

_____**When A Woman's Fed Up, $15 (April 2007)**
_____**Games Men Play, $15 (July 2007)**
_____**Love's Triangle, $15 (August)**
_____**Wolf In Sheep's Clothing, $15 (Sept. 2007)**
_____**Between Two Sisters, $15 (October, 2007)**

Also Available at bookstores everywhere.

<u>Use this coupon to order via mail</u>

Name_____
Address_____
City_____State_____
Zip Code_____

Shipping and Handling $5
Please allow 2-3 weeks for delivery.
        This offer subject to change without notice

Send checks or money orders to:

Bullet Entertainment Group
5441 Riverdale Rd. Suite 129
College Park, Ga 30349
www.Bentpublishing.com
Email: bulletent4000@yahoo.com

To order additional copies wholesale, please contact James Hickman at 404-246-6496 or bulletent4000@yahoo.com